MISSING!

Tracy looked at her friends. 'There's something wrong about this,' she said. 'Judy sounded kind of weird. And she asked about Harry.' She shook her head.

'Who is Harry?' asked Holly.

'He was my dog, when I was a kid,' said Tracy. 'Judy and I used to take him out together. But he got ill. Judy knows he got ill. She can't have forgotten.'

The other two girls waited while Tracy's mind went back to her childhood.

'Judy was with me. There's no way she could have forgotten. We sat up with him all night.' She looked with puzzled eyes at Holly and Belinda. 'The thing is,' she said, 'Harry died that night.'

'You're sure it was Judy with you?' asked Holly.

'Of *course* I'm sure,' said Tracy. ' Judy *knows* he's dead. So why should she ask me how he is? Unless —' She looked at her friends. 'Unless it was the only way she could let me know there's something wrong. Something really wrong with her down in London.'

The Mystery Club series

Missing!
The Mystery Club 6

Hodder
Children's
Books

a division of Hodder Headline plc

Hodder Children's Books
A Division of Hodder Headline plc
338 Euston Road
London NW1 3BH

1 A change of plan

'But I just can't manage!'

The Mystery Club heard Mrs Foster break off, sigh and continue listening to the voice at the other end of the telephone. As Tracy looked at her mother, Mrs Foster shrugged then spoke into the receiver.

'Judy will have to get the train by herself, I'm afraid. There's no way I can get down to London at such short notice.'

The determined voice squawked again.

'Yes, I know she's a capable girl. So long as you're quite happy with that arrangement.'

Tracy turned to her friends, Holly Adams and Belinda Hayes. 'My aunt,' she said ruefully.

The three members of the Mystery Club were all together in the sitting-room, eating biscuits and listening with interest to the long-distance telephone conversation between Tracy's mother and Tracy's American aunt.

The Mystery Club had started when Holly was new to Willow Dale. An advertisement in the school newspaper had produced remarkable results – not a flood of people, but instead two friends who not only shared Holly's love of ice-cream but also her passion for mystery stories. And there had been no shortage of real-life mysteries for them to sort out: danger and intrigue seemed to follow Holly and the Mystery Club wherever they went.

The voice on the other end of the telephone chattered again.

'If you'll just confirm the times . . . Yes . . . Yes, all right, Merrilyn, I suppose it would be more reasonable for me to find out from this end. I'll call you back.'

Mrs Foster slammed down the receiver and said crossly, 'Would you believe it! Merrilyn has changed her plans *again*. Judy is coming to-morrow instead of at the weekend. I simply can't change Fleur's hours again – she's put herself out too much as it is.' Fleur was Mrs Foster's assistant at the day nursery which she ran.

'Calm down, Mom,' said Tracy. She led her mother away from the telephone and made her sit down on the sofa. 'Tell us all about it, then I'll make some coffee. You look as if you need it.'

'It's just typical of your Aunt Merrilyn,' Mrs Foster began, exasperated. 'If only I'd had a bit more *notice*.'

'You can't go down to London to meet her?' guessed Holly, draping her slim body over an

2

armchair. 'No problem. It's half-term, so *we'll* go down instead.'

'No,' Mrs Foster said firmly. 'There's no reason why Judy shouldn't travel by herself to York. However, you could go to York and meet her there. I only said I'd go and collect her from Heathrow because I had to go down to London sooner or later and thought I might as well take the extra trip out to the airport. I can't afford to go twice, and there's no way Alan would be able to see me tomorrow at such short notice.'

Tracy grinned sympathetically at her mother. Mrs Foster periodically had to visit a member of the charity board, Alan Hargrave, in London and it was always a complicated operation to leave the nursery during weekdays.

'No problem,' declared Holly. 'We'll meet her in York and bring her back to Willow Dale on the local train.'

'Thank goodness for that,' said Belinda. Her eyes gleamed from behind her wire-framed spectacles. 'You two may find this hard to believe, but I'm not absolutely desperate to travel all the way to London *and* back again all in one day.'

The other two laughed. Belinda was well-known for her lack of energy. She would never take two steps where one would do, unless it was towards Meltdown, her chestnut thoroughbred.

'Right,' said Tracy in a businesslike way. 'Judy's plane lands at six fifty-five in the morning. It will take a couple of hours to get to King's Cross from Heathrow once she's picked up her baggage, so she could get a train to York about nine o'clock. I think I've got the current train timetable.'

'Do you ever *not* have a current timetable?' Holly said with a laugh. 'What else do you keep in that filing cabinet of yours?'

'Everything except her school work,' said Mrs Foster with some feeling. 'You would not believe, Holly, how hard I try to get her to be as efficient about her studies as she is about everything else!'

'I get by,' grinned Tracy.

'That's just my point,' began Mrs Foster. 'Still, this efficiency doesn't come from *my* side of the family.' Merrilyn may *seem* to be completely disorganised, but you can bet your boots she's got everything arranged right down to the last detail.' Merrilyn was Tracy's American father's sister. 'They're going on a touring holiday in the Catskill Mountains of Upstate New York and no one knows exactly where they'll be at any particular time. Your Uncle Jason will call us to make sure she's arrived safely.'

Mrs Foster sighed. 'I wish I could afford to disappear like that, even for a weekend! I never seem to be free of the nursery, even in holidays!' She laughed ruefully. 'I'll get back to my accounts, then, and thank you all. I don't know how I'd have managed without you.'

'Perfectly well, of course, like you always do,'

Tracy said fondly. She pushed her mother gently out of the sitting-room door. 'Go and do what you have to do, and leave everything else to us. I'll call Aunt Merrilyn back with instructions for Judy. You don't have to worry about a thing.' She turned back to her friends. 'It's going to be wonderful having Judy here. She was my best friend, you know, when we were young. We used to do everything together.'

Although Tracy had lived in Willow Dale with her English mother in the three years since her parents' divorce, it was clear to her friends that she still had a great love of the country where she had been born. Her voice always took on a stronger American accent whenever she talked of her life in California.

'Tell us more,' said Holly, settling herself more comfortably into the armchair, ready to listen intently. She couldn't help it – the subject could be trivial or complex, Holly would give it the same intense concentration. 'We want to know all about Judy and your aunt and uncle.'

'She's about my age,' began Tracy, and her pretty blue eyes took on a faraway expression. 'We were born in California, just streets away from each other. We were brought up practically as sisters, until Uncle Jason and Aunt Merrilyn moved over to New York. Uncle Jason runs a company which makes costume jewellery,' she explained. 'It's called Scheherazade. They sell to the big New York and Paris fashion houses. It's really big money nowadays. Nobody wants to drip with real diamonds and rubies any more, not in the fashion world.'

'I wouldn't mind,' said Holly, laughing.

'I can't see the point of all that jewellery anyway,' said Belinda. 'I'd feel a fool all dolled up like a Christmas tree.' As usual, Belinda was wearing a pair of old jeans and her favourite faded green sweat-shirt.

'I really missed her when they moved to the East Coast,' continued Tracy. 'We wrote, of course, and called each other, but it's not the same.'

Holly nodded sympathetically. Having only recently come to Willow Dale from London herself, she missed the friends she had been with since primary school, especially Miranda Hunt and Peter Hamilton. 'Letters are great,' she agreed, 'but it's not the same as actually being with your best friend.'

'The last time she wrote,' Tracy went on, 'they'd just finished their new collection, inspired by this fantastically ornate jewellery from Thailand. I think Uncle Jason actually borrowed some of the royal jewels to give them ideas for the designs. Judy says that Beaumont's, the big fashion house in Paris, was really interested in them.'

'Perhaps we'll be famous, just knowing her!' said Holly.

'It's not all fun,' Tracy told her. 'There was another thing Judy said – my uncle's sure someone is stealing their designs. You know, turning out similar designs and selling them to the big fashion houses before his are perfected. It's happened too often for it to be a coincidence, she says. My uncle's real worried about it. It looks like it could be someone in the company, so everybody's being suspicious of everyone else.'

'A real mystery!' began Holly with a gleam in her eye. But Belinda interrupted.

'Hey, I've got an idea!' she cried. 'You know my mother's charity parties? How about getting Judy to come and talk at one of them about her father's business? Mum's got a big do planned for this Saturday, and you know what they're like. She always invites local business people along.' Belinda grinned. 'They're the ones with the money. She's bound to have invited some jeweller's. The man who runs that big jeweller's in Market Street has been to a couple of my mother's parties. You know the shop I mean.'

'Medlock's?' said Holly.

'Yes, that's the one,' said Belinda. 'And there's at least three or four other jewellers' shops in town. They'll probably all be there. My mother's collecting for one of the children's charities. It might spur them on to pledge even more money if they know there's going to be a representative of a really famous American jewellers there.'

'Judy's not exactly a representative of Scheherazade,' said Tracy. 'And she's hardly going to give away the secrets of my uncle's new designs – not with Beaumont's of Paris ready to buy them. She'd be crazy to tell rival jeweller's what they're up to. New designs like that are worth a fortune.'

'But you said it's only costume jewellery,' said Belinda. 'It can't be worth *that* much, surely.'

Tracy gave Belinda a smile. 'You obviously don't know much about the jewellery business,' she said.

'And you do, I suppose?' said Belinda.

'I know that a new design from Scheherazade is worth a lot of money,' said Tracy. 'And I know Judy wouldn't tell anyone about them. My cousin's like a clam if she doesn't want you to know anything.'

'The people at the party won't know that,' said Belinda with a grin. 'So I can ask her, can I? Do you think Judy would be willing to make a little speech?'

'I'll ask,' said Tracy. 'Do I get to come as well?'

'Of course! I can't stand being at my mother's parties on my own. I'll get Mum to send you each an invitation.'

'Great – it sounds like fun!' declared Holly.

'You must be joking!' Belinda exclaimed with a shudder. 'I don't even want to think about it before I have to. Tell us more about Judy, Tracy. Anything to get my mind off my mother's awful party.'

'Well – she's pretty, she's clever, she's good at

athletics and tennis, she's got really good ideas for things to do – she used to tell me brilliant stories before we went to bed . . .'

'She sounds horribly like you,' said Belinda. 'No wonder you got on so well with her.'

'How long is it since you've seen her?' said Holly. 'She's probably changed a lot since you last met her. I bet you won't even recognise her when she steps on to that platform. You should have asked her to wear a label on her coat!'

'I get photographs, and she writes, like I said,' said Tracy. 'Of course I'll recognise her. I told you, we were inseparable when we were kids. But I haven't actually seen her in almost five years, not since she moved to New York.' A note of sadness crept into Tracy's voice.

Holly tactfully changed the subject. 'What I want to know is,' she said, 'why have your uncle and aunt gone away without leaving any address? That sounds pretty strange to me.'

'My parents' friends do that sort of thing all the time,' said Belinda. 'When you live in the public eye all year you want to get away from the press and creditors.'

'You think they owe money?' Holly said, her eyes gleaming.

'No!' said Belinda. 'Holly, you just can't resist making a mystery out of everything, can you? It's perfectly normal and reasonable.'

'It may be perfectly normal and reasonable to

you,' declared Holly, 'but it sounds very suspicious to me. Besides, it's been far too long since we had a good mystery to solve.'

'OK, OK, I admit it,' Tracy said, laughing. 'Uncle Jason is an industrial spy, and he's been sent off on a secret mission.'

'What about your aunt Merrilyn?' Holly put in quickly.

'Oh, she's been sent on the mission as well. International spies always have beautiful assistants.'

'You're both wrong, I know exactly what's happened,' Belinda said languidly. 'He's bored with his business so he's wound up everything and gone away to be an actor.'

'I doubt that,' said Holly. 'If you're an actor, you're going public in a big way. He couldn't hope not to be found out.'

Belinda shrugged. 'Maybe he's trying to prove himself as an unknown stage actor before he actually stars in a film.'

'I don't think my aunt Merrilyn would fall for that,' said Tracy. 'She's used to a pretty good standard of living. I can't see her agreeing to give all that up to follow my uncle around while he's playing at being a starving actor.'

'She's his manager, of course. And he's already secretly signed a deal with a big film company in Hollywood,' said Holly. 'My turn now. Maybe he's got involved with some drug barons, is being blackmailed and has got to go underground for a while.'

'With Aunt Merrilyn?' asked Belinda.

'She's the arch organiser,' said Holly quickly.

'What a pity it isn't any of these,' sighed Belinda. 'Haven't you got any good mysteries up your sleeve, Holly? As founder of the Mystery Club you ought to arrange something for us.'

'Well,' said Holly. 'I wouldn't mind having a go at figuring out who the person is who's stealing Tracy's uncle's designs.'

'Now that's a mystery!' Belinda exclaimed, 'Maybe we can even solve it before Judy arrives!'

'We'd better get organised on it now, then,' said Tracy. 'We've only got hours before she gets here.'

Holly laughed. 'And we'd really need to go to America if we're going to investigate properly. I don't suppose you've got the times of aeroplanes to New York in that filing cabinet of yours, Tracy?'

'I'm afraid not,' said Tracy. 'Still, it was a nice idea.'

'Oh, well,' said Holly. 'Back to the drawing board. Maybe you can use your organising genius to make sure we're in York at the right time to meet your cousin. She's not going to be very impressed if we're not there to meet her, is she?'

'Good idea,' said Tracy. She ran upstairs to find the train timetable from her bedroom. As soon as the three friends had made certain that they had the times of the trains from London to York

11

worked out, Tracy phoned her cousin and relayed times and connections to her.

Belinda raised her eyebrows at the furious chatter on the telephone. 'If she's going to be like this all the time Judy's here, I don't think I'm going to have the energy to keep up with them.' She looked at Holly. 'Can you imagine what it's going to be like to have *two* people like Tracy around?'

Holly grinned. 'If she doesn't get off the phone now Judy is going to miss that flight. I've never heard anyone talk so much!'

'More changes,' said Tracy when she came back from the telephone. Her American accent had deepened, as it always did whenever she was excited. 'She's travelling with one of my uncle's staff – a man called Tony Meyer. He's got business in London, apparently. Not that it makes any difference to us. We'll still meet her in York. I'm so excited. I don't know how I'm going to wait until tomorrow morning!'

Belinda and Holly exchanged a glance and smiled. Despite Belinda's wry comments, the two of them were looking forward to meeting Tracy's American cousin almost as much as Tracy was!

It seemed no time at all before they were standing by the barrier at York station, waiting for the London train to arrive. Tracy was still hyped up with excitement, jumping up and down like a nine year old.

They were too early, of course. Tracy had seen to that. They had taken a train from Willow Dale half an hour earlier than they needed, just in case Judy had found her luggage at lightning speed and been lucky with tube and train connections. The girls wandered round the kiosks along the platform, with Tracy talking non-stop, telling them about how well dressed and intelligent her cousin was until even Holly began to wonder if *anyone* could be that wonderful.

Belinda looked ruefully down at her favourite green sweat-shirt, which even she had to admit had seen better days, and felt that maybe she ought to have dressed up at least a little bit. The way Tracy was talking, it was as though they were about to meet royalty.

'I wonder if I'm going to like this marvellous cousin,' Belinda whispered to Holly while Tracy was restlessly scanning the Arrivals board.

'Tracy's just excited, that's all,' said Holly. 'I'd probably feel the same if Miranda or Peter came to visit.'

'Well, if she's as marvellous as Tracy makes out we should have a great time,' said Belinda. 'I wonder if she likes horses.'

'The train's coming,' shouted Tracy. 'Come on!' She grabbed an arm of each friend and hustled them to the platform. 'If we stand on each side of the barrier then we can't possibly miss her.'

There was no point protesting that they had

never seen the fabled Judy in their lives. Tracy simply told them to look for a five foot four American with blonde hair and enough baggage to stock a supermarket.

People streamed off the platform. It seemed as if the whole world was coming to York for the afternoon. There were exhausted mothers with children attached to push-chairs and cases; there were old people, pushing trolleys with a single light case perched on top; there were young couples with eyes only for each other; there were young men and young women anxiously scanning the barrier for the girlfriends or boyfriends they hoped were waiting for them; there were men swinging their briefcases ready for a business lunch. They all surged through the barrier, one by one, two by two, group by group, until the platform was completely empty but for a solitary guard, checking the carriages to see that everyone had got off the train.

But there was no sign of a blonde American, height five foot four, with enough baggage to stock a supermarket.

Where was Judy?

2 A strange message

'Trust Judy!' said Tracy irritably.

'Does she often do this?' asked Belinda.

'Miss trains? I don't know – I haven't seen her for years, I told you.'

Tracy was more upset than she wanted to admit. She had been so looking forward to her cousin's visit, and she didn't want her friends to think that Judy wasn't even capable of doing something as simple as catching a train. 'Oh, I suppose anyone can miss a train.'

'So what do we do?' said Belinda. 'Ring New York and ask if Judy caught the plane OK?'

'Have you got the phone number on you?' asked Holly.

'No,' admitted Tracy. 'I didn't think I'd need it. I could phone Mom for it.'

Holly could see her friend was too upset to think straight. 'Why don't we just wait for the next train,' she said soothingly. 'She's travelling with this friend of her father's, you said. What was his name? Tony Meyer? If there's anything really wrong he'll have telephoned your home. If she's not on the next train we can phone your mum then. How's that?'

'OK. Right,' agreed Tracy, although it was quite clear she was still terribly nervous. However, after a Coke in the station buffet she relaxed enough to laugh. 'Sorry I got so upset,' she said. 'I just felt so responsible. If I'd seen Judy more recently, I don't think I'd be so worried. But you know how it is – you wonder how much people will have changed. To be honest,' she said, 'I wondered whether I'd still recognise her. You know what it's like if people have their hair different and so on.'

'I know exactly what you mean,' declared Belinda. 'My mother sent me to meet an uncle I hadn't seen since I was about two. As far as she was concerned he hadn't changed a bit. I still remembered him looking like a pirate – about ten foot tall, with black hair and a huge beard.'

'What was he really like?' asked Holly.

'He'd shaved off his beard, his hair was grey and he wasn't much bigger than me,' admitted Belinda. 'I was really quite disappointed. He looked like an ordinary man, and not like a pirate at all.'

'That doesn't make me feel any better,' said Tracy. 'What if Judy was on that train? What if I really didn't recognise her and she walked straight past us?'

'I don't believe that happened for a moment,' said Holly reassuringly. 'The only young people I

16

saw definitely had people to meet them.'

'What if she caught the early train – the eight o'clock!' Tracy exclaimed. 'Suppose the plane was early, and she got to King's Cross in time to catch the train before the one she was supposed to be on?'

'Then she'll be wandering around the station,' said Belinda. 'Or she could be somewhere nearby having a cup of coffee or something. Come on, you two, a prize for the first to spot her.'

They scoured the station, looking into every snack bar and shop, but the only blonde of roughly the right height and age was having a row with her boyfriend, and she had a very definite English accent.

Tracy began to look worried again. 'I *told* her we'd meet her. She wouldn't have gone to Willow Dale on her own. Even if she asked someone how to get there, she wouldn't just wander off when she knew we were coming here to meet her.' She looked anxiously at her friends. 'Suppose she's had an accident and—'

Holly interrupted her. 'When did you say the next train came in, Tracy?'

It was a good move. Tracy immediately stopped inventing disasters for her cousin and became efficient once again. 'Twenty minutes,' she said, running her finger down the column of the train schedule.

'Time for another Coke and a wander round the

bookshop,' decided Holly. She and Belinda exchanged a glance. *Keep her busy*, it said.

But twenty minutes later the next train arrived, and once more Judy wasn't on it. The three friends were at a loss what to do.

'I've had enough Coke to last me a lifetime,' said Belinda. 'We can't really wait around for the *next* train, surely?'

'And I think I know the front cover of every book and magazine by heart,' said Holly. 'The plane was probably late – they always are.' She nodded reassuringly at Tracy. 'That'll be what's happened,' she said. 'Some hold-up at the airport.'

'I'll call Mom,' said Tracy. 'There could be a message. We should have done that before.'

'Perhaps she's lost her luggage,' said Belinda as they walked towards the phone booths. 'Maybe she's standing around in Heathrow and all her luggage is on a plane to China.' She glanced at Holly, hoping their inventions were helping to calm Tracy down.

'Suppose Judy got off at the wrong station?' asked Tracy.

'She's not that silly, surely,' said Holly. 'Really, there'll be nothing to worry about. There's always an explanation.'

As they waited by the phone booths till one was free Holly and Belinda tried to reassure Tracy with stories about the number of people that they had been to meet from airports and stations only to find that the train or plane had been hours late.

'No message,' said Tracy flatly after she had put down the receiver.

'That proves it,' said Belinda. 'She must still be on the plane.'

'Or she's stuck on a train held up halfway between Selby and Nottingham,' suggested Holly.

'They'd have announced that,' said Tracy. 'Nobody's said anything about delayed trains.'

'Then how about phoning the airport to see if the plane has landed?' suggested Belinda.

'Good thing someone's got brains,' said Holly.

But that drew a blank too. The aircraft had landed if not dead on time at least within enough minutes of its scheduled time for both Judy and her companion to have taken the tube from Heathrow and easily caught either of the trains the Mystery Club had met.

'She's either missed it in New York or she's sightseeing in London,' said Belinda.

'She wouldn't do that,' Tracy said emphatically. 'Sightseeing? When she knows we're here to meet her? Talk sense!'

'I'm only trying to be helpful,' said Belinda. 'Don't bite my head off.'

'I'm sorry,' said Tracy. 'I'm really worried. If she'd missed the plane either she or this Tony Meyer guy she's travelling with would have called my mom by now. And she'd never go sightseeing and miss two trains without saying. She's not that sort of person.'

'We've got to make some decision,' said Holly. 'Do we stay here or go back home and wait for a call?'

'Or wait for the next train, *then* go back and see if there's been a message,' said Belinda.

'She won't have got lost in the London Underground, I suppose?' asked Holly. 'It's pretty complicated for someone who's never been there before.'

'I gave her *all* the directions she needed. She couldn't possibly have got lost,' said Tracy, upset. 'She's not stupid,' she added. Then, urgently, 'I've got a funny feeling about this. I think I'd rather go back home now, just in case she calls.'

'I'm certain she'll call,' said Holly. 'There's some simple explanation behind this, I'm sure.'

They were a silent trio on the train back to Willow Dale. Rain dripped down the windows, adding to their gloomy mood, and clouds hung down like grey curtains. They just missed a bus back to Tracy's house so they walked, wet and miserable, to the nursery, where there was still no message. And Mrs Foster was too busy with a homesick three year old and the feeding of two babies to share Tracy's worries at that particular moment.

'There must be some explanation – there always is,' she said. 'Go and get yourselves some lunch.

I'm just sorry you've had a wasted morning.'

They went into the kitchen. Tracy searched the fridge for something warming to cheer them up.

'I could do with something to soak up all that Coke!' declared Belinda. 'I'm bloated.'

'It serves you right if you've got a stomach ache,' said Holly. 'I don't know where you put it all.'

'I like Coke,' said Belinda, clutching her stomach. 'At least, I did up until the third can.' She grinned at Tracy, hoping her joke was taking her friend's mind off her worries. 'I never thought I'd get sick of it. I don't suppose there's any chance of a sandwich or two?'

'I'll see what there is,' said Tracy. Then suddenly the telephone shrilled and she froze.

'Do you think?'

'Answer it,' said Holly. 'Come on. Quick!'

Tracy ran and picked up the receiver.

'Hello? Tracy Foster speaking.'

It wasn't Judy. It was a man. A man with an American accent.

'Tracy! Hi! This is Tony Meyer,' said the voice down the phone.

Tracy almost fell over with relief. 'Is everything OK?' she gasped. 'Is Judy all right? We waited for hours but she never turned up.'

'Everything's just fine,' said Tony Meyer. 'Judy's with me now. There's been a change of plan.' He gave a laugh. 'We'd have phoned before, but Judy had packed your phone number at the bottom of

21

one of her bags. It's taken us all this time to find it. I'm sorry you had a wasted journey.'

'I don't care about *that*,' said Tracy. 'I was worried that something had happened.'

'No. Nothing's happened. We'll be staying in London for a few days, that's all. Oh, and another thing. Let me give you a number to ring if you need to get a message to Judy's folks.'

'Just a second,' said Tracy, hunting for a slip of paper. 'OK,' she said. 'Fire away.' She wrote down the long phone number.

'Could I have a quick word with Judy, please?' asked Tracy.

'One moment,' said Tony Meyer. 'I'll get her for you.'

Tracy put her hand over the receiver, smiling with relief at her two friends. 'It's all OK,' she said. 'They're still in London.'

'What did we tell you?' said Holly. 'All that panic for nothing.'

'Tracy?' a girl's voice sounded down the phone. Tracy nodded at her friends. She recognised Judy's voice straight away.

'Judy! It's great to hear you. You'll never—'

'I can't talk now,' interrupted Judy. Tracy thought she sounded tired. 'We'll be stopping here for a few days. Something's come up.'

'But I thought—' began Tracy.

'I'll come on to you as soon as I can, I promise. I'll call again when I know exactly what I'm doing.'

'But why didn't you—' began Tracy again.

'By the way, how's Harry?' Judy said.

'Harry?' Tracy's startled eyes turned to her friends.

'Sure. Harry. I'm really looking forward to seeing him again. Look, I have to go now. I'll be in touch soon. Bye.'

And then Tracy heard the buzz that told her Judy had put down the receiver.

'Something's come up,' Tracy said to her friends in a bewildered voice. 'But she didn't say what.'

'You should have asked her,' said Belinda.

'I tried to,' said Tracy. 'She said she couldn't talk. I don't get it.'

'It must be OK,' said Holly. 'If she's with that business friend of your uncle's.'

Tracy looked at her friends. 'There's something wrong about this,' she said. 'She sounded, I don't know, she sounded kind of weird. And she asked about Harry.' She shook her head. 'I don't get it.'

'Who is Harry?' asked Holly.

'That's what's so strange,' Tracy said blankly. 'She asked me how Harry was.'

'For heaven's sake,' said Belinda. 'Who *is* Harry?'

'He was my dog, when I was a kid,' said Tracy. 'We used to take him out together, me and Judy. He was a Great Dane, a lovely old Great Dane. But he got ill. She knows he got ill. She can't have forgotten.'

The other two girls waited while Tracy's mind went back to her childhood.

'Judy was with me. We were both ten. It was only weeks before Judy's family moved away. There's no way she could have forgotten. We sat up with him all night.' She looked with anxious, puzzled eyes at her two friends. 'The thing is,' she said, 'Harry died that night.'

'You're sure it was Judy with you?' asked Holly.

'Of *course* I'm sure,' said Tracy. 'You don't forget things like that. Judy *knows* he's dead. So why should she ask me how he is? It doesn't make sense. Unless—' She looked at her friends. 'Unless it was the only way she could let me know there's something wrong. Something really wrong with her down in London.'

3 'Keep these to yourself'

'I don't think we need worry about her,' said Mrs Foster, when Tracy told her about the phone call. 'I do think she could have let us know sooner, but at least she's telephoned to apologise. I expect that Tony Meyer's keeping an eye on her. Perhaps he had some business down there and she's staying on with him to have a look round the city.'

'I suppose so,' said Tracy. 'But that doesn't explain her asking about Harry.'

'She's got muddled,' said Mrs Foster. 'She was always a bit scatter-brained, as I remember. If she's with Tony she'll be fine. Come on, Tracy, he's been with your uncle's firm for years. He'll make sure she comes to no harm.'

But Tracy was still unsure. Could Judy really have forgotten what happened with Harry?

'Could we telephone just to be certain?' she pleaded. 'Aunt Merrilyn and Uncle Jason might still be there.'

'You could try,' said Mrs Foster. 'If it'll put your mind at rest. But they'll only confirm what you've already been told: Judy and Tony Meyer are staying in London for a few days, and she'll be up later in the week. But go ahead and phone, if you want to. And you tell them from me that these last-minute changes of plan are a pain in the neck.'

Tracy dialled the home phone number in New York.

'It's a recorded message,' she said shortly. 'Nobody's there.'

'There you are,' said Mrs Foster. 'They've gone off on their holidays already.'

'I could try the phone number Tony Meyer gave me,' said Tracy.

'That was only for an emergency, Tracy,' said Mrs Foster. 'They're not going to thank you for bothering them when we already know what's happened. Look, I know you and your friends like mysteries, but I'm not having you spending money on international phone calls when there's no mystery at all.'

'No, you're right,' said Tracy. 'It was just an idea, that's all. And Uncle Jason will be phoning us soon anyway, to make sure she's arrived safely.'

'Exactly,' said her mother.

There was no point in worrying her mother any more — or worrying *herself* for that matter. Judy had telephoned. She was with Tony Meyer. There wasn't anything wrong. The strange edge to Judy's voice was probably nothing more sinister than jet-lag. All that Tracy could do was wait for another call from Judy, telling her when she would be coming up.

It was disappointing to think she had to wait even longer to see her cousin, but Tracy felt sure Judy would explain everything once she finally arrived in Willow Dale.

Uncle Jason telephoned later that night to check that Judy had arrived safely.

'I – I don't understand,' Tracy stammered into the phone. 'I thought *you'd* know why they stayed in London.'

'Tony had business there,' said Tracy's uncle. 'That's why he's there. But Judy said nothing to us about wanting to spend a few days there with him. But if she's phoned and she's with him, there's nothing to worry about. Judy's got her vacation allowance, so she's not short of money. I guess she'll come to Willow Dale after she's seen all the sights. You know what it's like when you're in a big city. Plenty to look at.'

'If you're sure . . .' Tracy said uncertainly.

'You don't sound convinced,' said her uncle. 'Look, Tracy, Tony Meyer is one of my oldest and most trusted friends. If she's with him she'll be fine.'

'I guess so,' said Tracy, calmed by the assurance in her uncle's voice. 'How's the vacation going?'

Her uncle chuckled. 'I'm having a whale of a time,' he said. 'But your aunt is finding it all a bit of a strain. She likes having her home conveniences around her. I don't think she's too happy about us living in a camper for two weeks. You know what she's like.' His laughter rang cheerily down the wires. 'She'll get used to it. Look, I'd better go now. I'll give it a couple of days, and then I'll ring to check Judy's arrived with you in one piece. OK?'

'Yes, fine. Give my love to Aunt Merrilyn,' said Tracy.

'I'll do that. And you've got my permission to tell Judy off for stringing you along like this.'

'How do I contact you if there are any problems?' asked Tracy.

'You've got the New York number. They'll get a message to us. Bye, Tracy. And don't worry about Judy. She can look after herself.'

The phone went dead.

'And that was it,' Tracy said to her friends. 'He said she'd be fine.'

'There you are then,' said Holly. 'If even her father isn't worried, there's certainly no reason for you to carry on fretting about her.'

'I know, I know,' said Tracy. 'But I still can't get it out of my head that she asked about Harry. And her voice sounded so strange.'

'Jet-lag,' said Belinda. 'And your imagination running riot.'

'Jet-lag doesn't make you forget things,' Tracy

insisted. 'I don't care what anyone says. My mom might think she's scatter-brained, and my uncle might think she's down in London sightseeing, but I'm telling you, there's something screwy about all this. I don't know what, but I'm really certain there's something wrong.'

'Like what?' asked Holly.

'I don't know.' Tracy looked pleadingly at her two friends. 'It's driving me crazy,' she said. 'Nobody believes me.'

'But even if you're right,' Belinda said dubiously. 'What are we supposed to do about it? Do you want us to rush down to London and check it out? We don't even know where she's staying, for heaven's sake.'

'Yes. And that's another thing,' Tracy said in a rush. 'Why didn't she say where they were staying? And why couldn't she tell me why she'd decided not to come straight up?'

'She's sightseeing,' Belinda said tiredly.

'But she didn't *say* that,' Tracy insisted. 'She said she couldn't talk. Why not?'

'Perhaps that Tony Meyer was holding a gun at her head,' said Belinda.

Tracy stared at her.

'I was joking,' said Belinda. 'Who knows why she couldn't talk right then? Perhaps she was on a pay phone. Perhaps they had to go out somewhere? There's loads of reasons, and not one of them needs to be in the least bit sinister.'

'Belinda's right,' said Holly. 'Look, your uncle said he'd phone in a couple of days, right? Well, if you haven't heard anything from Judy by then, you can tell him. He'll know what to do. He'll be able to get in contact with this Tony Meyer guy, won't he?'

Tracy looked from one friend to the other. 'OK,' she said slowly. 'Maybe I am completely wrong. But I'm telling you one thing – if I haven't heard from Judy in two days I'm getting on to the police.' She frowned at the exasperated expressions on Holly's and Belinda's faces. 'And I don't care what anyone says.'

A parcel arrived at the Fosters' house first post the following morning. It was addressed to Tracy, with a smudgy postmark that was impossible to decipher.

She tore off the wrappings, puzzled as to who could have sent her the package. It wasn't her birthday, and she hadn't sent away for anything.

It was a box of chocolates. A large white box, with a huge glossy ribbon tied diagonally across it. The gilt-edged label said that there were two enticing layers of exciting dark chocolates inside. Two layers of dark chocolates with exotic fillings.

Tracy stared at it.

No one who knew her would send her dark chocolates. Everyone who even remotely knew her would be aware that she didn't like dark chocolate.

Who on earth . . .? Tracy said to herself.

Tucked into the ribbon was a note. In familiar handwriting. 'Keep these to yourself,' it said.

It was signed 'Judy'.

'There, she feels really bad about letting us down,' said Mrs Foster when Tracy showed her the box. 'She does have good manners after all.'

'But I don't like dark chocolates, Mom,' said Tracy. 'She knows I don't.'

'It's the thought that counts,' said Mrs Foster. 'Perhaps that was the only box she could find.' She shrugged. 'It's a pity, though. I can't stand dark chocolate either.'

'What am I supposed to do with them?' said Tracy.

'There's bound to be someone you know who'll eat them. What about Belinda? She'll eat anything.'

Tracy frowned. 'If this is Judy's idea of making up for staying down in London, it's a pretty poor one,' she said.

This strange present was very puzzling.

In fact, the more Tracy thought about it, the more puzzling the whole thing became. During the morning as she did the chores for her mother, she kept looking at Judy's note, taking it out of its ribbon and putting it back in again.

Was it simply good manners as her mother had said? Or was this another way that Judy had found to try and tell Tracy something? Something like

31

her comment about Harry. Something that only Tracy would understand. Except that Tracy *didn't* understand. She didn't understand at all.

By mid-afternoon Tracy was so confused that all she could think of was to phone Holly. OK, so Belinda and Holly had been unconvinced by her worries. But now there were *two* strange things to think about.

'I've had something peculiar from Judy in the mail,' she said immediately as Holly answered the phone. 'I really need to talk about it.'

'A ransom note?' asked Holly, her voice sounding amused.

'It's not funny,' said Tracy. 'I want to talk to you about it.'

'Come right over,' said Holly. 'In fact, do one better than that. Why don't you come over for the afternoon and dinner? You can stay the night, too. That would be fun! I'm cooking and I could use some help! We'll ask Belinda too. Then we can have a proper Mystery Club meeting. We might as well enjoy ourselves over half-term, even if Judy isn't going to be here for a few days. And if Judy phones while you're out, your mum can ring here and let you know.'

'Yes, I'll do that,' Tracy said, relaxing a little. 'Maybe it would be a good idea. Otherwise I'm just standing by the phone, waiting.'

'At least if you've got something from her you know she's all right,' said Holly.

'I'm not so sure,' said Tracy. 'I'll explain when I get there. I'll see you in a few minutes.'

'I'll phone Belinda and ask her to come right now,' Holly said.

'Yes, if you can drag her away from her afternoon ride on Meltdown!'

'I'll promise her some ice-cream,' Holly joked. 'That usually works.'

After she'd hung up the phone, Tracy took the note out of the box of chocolates and put it in her pocket.

'Have a good time,' said Mrs Foster when Tracy told her their plans for the night. 'Why don't you take those chocolates along for Holly's mum? A thank-you present for letting you stay?'

'Yes,' said Tracy. 'That's a good idea. It'd be a shame to waste them.' She tucked the curious present under her arm and set off for Holly's house.

The day was crisp and bright after the rain. The threatening grey skies had turned to a pale, washed blue and what clouds remained were white and puffy. Belinda, despite her lazy image, had been out since mid-morning and had gone for a ride into the hills. The becks were full and gurgling from the flood water which rushed down from the high ground. Meltdown's hooves had thrown up great splashes of mud and Belinda's jodhpurs had taken on strange streaky designs as she'd forged through the puddles.

Her friends had barely had time for a first helping of raspberry ice-cream before Belinda arrived, breathless not only from her ride but from the journey across town on her mountain bike.

'Look at this mess!' she exclaimed, trying to brush off a sticky white, limy mud which had splashed on to her brown jodhpurs. 'Next time I'll keep to the fields. This stuff is lethal!'

'Where did it come from?' asked Holly. 'It's not normal mud colour at all.'

'I went exploring. There are a lot of big empty houses around. There was one I found today that had its drive full of puddles of this stuff! Hey, leave some for me, you two!' she protested, seeing the empty ice-cream carton on the kitchen table.

'Don't worry, there's plenty more,' laughed Holly, going to the freezer for a fresh pack. 'Tracy's had a parcel in the post this morning,' she said, spooning ice-cream into a bowl.

'From Judy,' Tracy told Belinda. 'Chocolates. Here's the message.' She passed the note over to Belinda.

'From New York?' Belinda asked, swallowing a spoonful of ice-cream. 'Something she posted off before she left?'

'No,' said Tracy. 'I can't read the postmark, but it's from England. It's got a British stamp. That means she's posted them since she arrived.'

'Oh, I get it,' said Belinda. 'To say sorry for

34

messing us about.' She looked at the box. 'Dark chocolates?' she said. 'You don't like them, do you?'

'No, I don't,' said Tracy. 'That's the whole point. Judy knows I don't like them. It's some sort of message, I'm sure of it. Just like when she mentioned Harry.' She looked determinedly at her friends. 'She's trying to tell me something.'

'OK,' Holly said, taking out the Mystery Club's red notebook. 'Let's write down all your reasons for thinking something's happened to Judy. One at a time.'

'Thank heavens you're finally beginning to believe me,' said Tracy.

'I'm not sure I am,' said Holly. 'But if you're convinced there's something up, we ought at least to discuss it logically.' She shifted the carton of ice-cream to make room to write. With a ball-point pen poised, she said, 'Point one: Judy doesn't arrive in York when she's supposed to, though the plane and the trains were all on time.'

Belinda carried on, 'Two, she phones Tracy and asks about a dog she should know has died.'

'Point three, and this is really important,' said Tracy, 'Judy doesn't behave like this. I know her. I can't believe she's let us down just to go sightseeing. I know teenagers are supposed to be pretty irresponsible, but Judy was really looking forward to seeing me again. This just isn't like her.'

'That's a good point,' Holly said decidedly, and

35

wrote it down. 'Now, point four – Tracy's parcel this morning. A box of dark chocolates, posted in England after she'd landed.'

'Which could be a thank-you present,' said Belinda.

'Not when she knows I don't like dark chocolates,' Tracy insisted.

'Is there anything else?' asked Holly.

'No,' said Tracy. 'That's it.'

'OK,' said Holly. 'And now we write down the reasons why we *don't* think anything's happened to her.'

'She phoned,' said Belinda. 'And she's with this Tony Meyer.'

'A trusted employee of your uncle,' said Holly, writing.

Belinda spooned up some ice-cream. 'And your uncle says she'll be fine with him,' she said. She looked at the box of chocolates. 'I wish people would let me down and then send me boxes of chocolates.' She sighed.

'You're not getting them,' said Tracy, 'so you can stop looking. I'm going to give them to Holly's mom when she gets home.' She looked over Holly's shoulder. 'That's all the positive points we've got,' she said. 'And I'm still not convinced.'

'I've always found,' said Holly, 'that if you can't come up with a solution to a problem, the best bet is to think about something else for a while.'

'Meaning what?' asked Tracy.

'Meaning I've offered to cook dinner for everyone tonight, and you two can help me,' Holly said with a grin.

'Is it OK for me to phone home?' asked Tracy later that afternoon. 'You never know – Judy might have been in touch already.'

'Go ahead,' said Holly. They had all but finished the preparations for the meal. 'Belinda! Are you nibbling again?'

'No,' Belinda said guiltily, putting a fork down. 'I was just checking that everything was all right.'

Tracy came back from her phone call. There had been no message from Judy. Mrs Foster had promised to give Tracy a ring the moment she heard anything.

'I think I ought to go home,' said Tracy. 'Just in case.'

'In case of what?' asked Holly.

'I don't know. In case Judy phones and says something that only I'll understand.' She sat dejectedly at the table. 'It's very difficult when no one believes you,' she said.

Belinda put an arm around her. 'We believe you,' she said. 'And if we haven't heard anything by tomorrow, we could always go along to the police.'

Tracy looked up at her. 'Yes,' she said. 'I think that's exactly what we should do.'

Just then Mrs Adams walked in from her day at

the bank where she worked as a manager.

Holly's mother exclaimed with delight at the box of chocolates. 'What a kind thought. And all dark chocolate, too. How did you know they were my favourites, Tracy?'

'Just a lucky guess,' said Tracy with a smile.

'I'm going to keep these for when I've got time to put my feet up and watch a good movie on television,' said Mrs Adams.

There was a thunder of feet along the hall and Holly's younger brother, Jamie, came cannoning into the kitchen.

'Is the food ready yet?' he asked.

'It will be in ten minutes,' said Holly.

'Right,' said Mrs Adams. 'Jamie, you wash your hands, and then you can go down and tell your father dinner's ready. Tell him Holly and the girls have been cooking, and if he isn't at the table in ten minutes we'll eat it all.' She smiled at the three girls. 'That might make him come quicker.'

Mr Adams, once a lawyer but now a successful carpenter of hand-crafted furniture, had turned to his new trade in order to have more time with his family. But sometimes Mr Adams got so involved with his beautiful furniture that he spent long hours in the workshop and frequently had to be called for mundane things like dinner.

Jamie came back dragging his father by the arm. 'I thought this was the best way to get him,' he said, grinning. 'Dad, I think you should test the food first.'

'Test?' said Holly. 'Don't you mean taste?'

'No, test,' repeated Jamie. 'If you've made it, somebody's got to try it first. I don't want to be poisoned.'

'Very funny,' said Holly. 'Pest. No one's going to force you to eat it. There's plenty of dry bread in the bin.'

Mr Adams made up for Jamie's insult by complimenting the girls on their cooking.

After the meal, Mr Adams collared Jamie to help with the washing-up, while Mrs Adams went to watch some television and the three girls went up to Holly's room.

'I wonder if Judy's phoned,' said Tracy. 'What if she phoned and my mom didn't hear it?'

'You're really jumpy about all this, aren't you?' Holly said to her friend. 'You're even beginning to make me think there must be something wrong.'

'Let's worry about it in the morning,' said Belinda, stretching herself out on Holly's bed. 'I'm too full and comfortable for any mysteries now.'

'Let's talk about what we can do once Judy gets here,' said Holly.

'*If* she gets here,' said Tracy.

She sounded so depressed that Holly jumped up to put one of Tracy's favourite tapes into the cassette player.

The tape had only played halfway through the

second song when Jamie thumped at the door.

'Tracy!' he shouted. 'Telephone! Your mum!'

Tracy looked round at her friends with a sudden bright smile on her face. 'Judy!' she said, and almost ran out of Holly's room.

When Tracy returned her face was ashen.

'M – my mother was called away from home,' she stammered. 'And when she got back someone had ransacked the house! I've got to go there. I've got to go there right away!'

4 The clue in the chocolate box

The girls looked at one another in horror.

'Why should anyone burgle us?' Tracy cried. 'We haven't got anything valuable. Mom said they've pulled all the drawers out and been through all the cupboards. The place is a complete mess. My poor mom – she must be going crazy over there on her own. I've got to get back to her.'

'Bad news, Tracy?' Mrs Adams was passing with an armful of papers.

Tracy turned to her. 'We've been burgled!' she cried. 'I'm just going.'

'Burgled! That's terrible! Is there anything I can do?' Mrs Adams asked, her voice full of concern. 'Wait one second for me to get my coat and I'll drive you round.'

'We'll come too,' declared Holly. 'We can help clear up. Has your mum phoned the police?'

'I didn't think to ask!' Tracy exclaimed. 'I'd better call Mom back and see if she's—'

'Tracy,' Mrs Adams said gently, 'your mother will have already thought of that. She'll have dealt with everything, you'll see.'

41

Tracy looked a little shamefaced. 'Sorry,' she said. 'You're right. It was just the thought of Mom being there all on her own.' She frowned. 'I *knew* I should have gone home. I must have known something like this was going to happen.'

Mrs Adams smiled, patted Tracy on the shoulder and led them out to the car.

She parked between two police cars outside the Fosters' terraced house.

'Is there anything I can do to help?' Mrs Adams asked when Mrs Foster came to the door, shocked and unnerved.

Mrs Foster shook her head. 'It's not the mess – we can soon clear that up. It's the thought of someone poking about amongst my things!' Mrs Foster said, showing them into the house and waving an arm dramatically at her sitting room.

They had never seen anything like it. The contents of all the drawers were tipped out on the floor. Even the cushions had been torn from the seats. It looked like a disaster area.

Tracy rushed to hug her mother. 'What happened?' she cried. 'How did they get in?'

'There was a phone call,' said Mrs Foster. 'Someone rang me and said you'd been involved in an accident and that you were in hospital. So I just dropped everything.' She ran her fingers through her hair. 'But when I got to the hospital they didn't know anything about it. And when I got back home I found *this*.'

42

'They lured you away,' Holly gasped, her eyes round. 'They deliberately made sure the house was empty.'

Mrs Foster sat down on the edge of the coffee table, her knees suddenly shaking. 'It's a wicked thing to do,' she said, holding Tracy's hands. 'As if *this* weren't bad enough. To frighten me like that as well.'

'There are some nasty people about,' said Mrs Adams. 'Did they take much? Have you had time to look?'

Mrs Foster gave a choking laugh. 'So far as I can see they didn't take anything at all. The television's still here. So is the video. All the things you'd expect them to run off with. It's almost as if they just broke in to smash the place up.'

Tracy picked up a cushion and put it back on the sofa.

'Tracy, don't!' began Holly, but Mrs Foster interrupted.

'It's all right,' said Mrs Foster. 'The police have finished in here.' She looked up at Tracy. 'I'm afraid it's even worse upstairs,' she said. 'Your room in particular, Tracy. Every single drawer has been opened, our wardrobes have been completely cleared out and the clothes thrown all over the place. As for the kitchen . . .' She shook her head. 'It's very kind of you to offer to help,' she added to Mrs Adams. 'But there's really nothing you can do at the moment. The police are still

43

taking photographs in the rest of the house, and I can't touch anything until they've finished. Tracy will help me clear up when they've gone.' She turned to Tracy, her voice shaking. 'This is a pretty poor end to your evening, isn't it, honey?'

'Don't worry about me,' said Tracy. 'It's you who needs looking after.'

'We could stay,' said Belinda. 'To help clear up, once the police have finished.'

'You're very kind,' said Mrs Foster. 'I hardly know where to begin.'

'I'll pick Holly and Belinda up later,' said Mrs Adams. She rested a hand on Mrs Foster's shoulder. 'Just let me know if there's anything I can do.'

As the girls were helping to put things back in their places in the sitting-room a police sergeant poked his head round the door. 'We'll be off now,' he said. 'If you could make a list of what seems to be missing, Mrs Foster, we'll be in touch. I know it won't be of any comfort to you, but we're pretty sure this was amateurs. Young lads out for what they could get. Professionals don't make this sort of mess.'

'Can I go up to my room now?' asked Tracy.

The police officer nodded.

The three friends made their way upstairs. They stared in through the doorway of Tracy's bedroom. Mrs Foster hadn't been exaggerating when she'd told them things were worse up here.

Even Tracy's bed had been upended, and her

44

filing cabinet was lying on its side with all its drawers hanging open and all her precious papers scattered over the carpet.

'I can't stand it!' shouted Tracy. 'Look at it! Just look at it!' She burst into tears.

Holly put her arm around her shoulders. 'Why don't you go down and help your mother? We'll start tidying up in here.'

'No,' said Tracy, anger overcoming her tears. 'You won't know where everything should go. I think it'd be better if you two went and helped my mom.' She looked grimly at all the chaos. 'If I ever catch the people responsible for this . . .' she whispered, letting her voice trail off.

Belinda and Holly trailed unhappily downstairs. They heard Mrs Foster clearing up in the kitchen.

They went into the sitting-room.

Holly looked out of the window and frowned. 'That's funny,' she said.

'What is?' asked Belinda.

'That car. See it?'

Belinda looked out into the darkened street. On the far side of the road a green car was parked with its lights off, but with someone clearly sitting at the wheel. They could even see the pale shape of a face peering towards them through the side window.

'What of it?' said Belinda. 'It's probably just some nosy passer-by. You know what people are like when they see police cars. They've always got time to have a good look at what's going on.'

'He's been here since we arrived,' said Holly. 'I noticed it when we got out of Mum's car.'

'A reporter, then?' Belinda suggested. 'From a local newspaper?'

'So why hasn't he come over?' said Holly. She walked towards the door. 'I'm going to have a word with him.'

Belinda watched through the sitting-room window as the light from the Fosters' opened front door spilled out on the path.

She saw Holly march out on to the pavement. The lights of the car suddenly blazed and Belinda heard the motor rev. With a skid of wheels the car drove away.

Holly came back into the sitting-room.

'You frightened him off,' said Belinda. 'Did you get a look at him?'

'No. But I got the number plate, just in case.' She pulled out her notebook and jotted the number down. 'And there was a sticker in the back window. A checked design. I'd better make a note of that as well. Oh, and the wheels were odd as well. They looked white.'

'But he can't have been anything to do with the burglary, surely?' said Belinda. 'Why would he still be hanging about?'

'I'm not suggesting he is,' said Holly. 'But if he's been out there for a while he might have seen something. At least we could give the registration number to the police. You never know.'

The two girls did the best they could in the sitting-room and then went back up to see how Tracy was getting on.

Holly told her about the car, but Tracy was too preoccupied to take much notice. She, like Belinda, guessed that it was just a nosy passer-by enjoying the show.

'It's horrible the way people like to see other people in trouble,' she said, picking up a pile of papers and throwing them down on her desk.

'Is anything missing?' asked Belinda.

'No. I don't think so,' said Tracy. 'What on earth can they have been up to? What were they looking for? There's nothing valuable here. It's not even as if my mom's got a box of jewellery or anything.'

'But you've got a point,' said Holly. 'It really is as if they were looking for something. Something specific. Something that could be hidden in a drawer or under a pile of clothes.'

'Do you think someone *told* them there was something here?' Belinda suggested.

'Like what?' said Tracy.

Holly gave a gasp and grabbed Tracy's arm. 'Like a small package,' she said. 'Like the package you got from Judy.'

Holly's brain was working quickly now. 'Look, what if you were right all along,' she said as her two friends stared open-mouthed at her. 'What if something *has* happened to Judy? What if she put

47

a message *in* the box of chocolates? And what if the people who've got her found out that she sent the box? What would they do?'

'What people?' said Tracy. 'She's with Tony Meyer.'

'Is she though?' said Holly. 'You wouldn't know his voice, would you? It could have been anyone speaking to you on the phone. For all we know they might have her and Tony Meyer.'

Tracy frowned. 'I don't know, Holly . . .'

'Neither do I,' said Holly. 'But there's one way to find out. And that's by looking in the box of chocolates. If I'm wrong, there'll be nothing there.'

'But if you're right,' said Belinda. 'It would mean Tracy's been on the right track all along.' She looked at Holly. 'We've got to get that box back from your mother.'

'No problem,' said Holly. 'I'll ring home now and get her to pick us up.' She looked at Tracy. 'And we'll phone you if we find anything.'

But it wasn't Mrs Adams who came to pick the two girls up. It was Holly's father.

'Your mother has fallen asleep in front of the television,' he explained. 'I didn't have the heart to wake her up.'

'Has she opened the chocolates?' asked Holly.

'What chocolates?' asked Mr Adams.

Holly shook her head. 'Never mind,' she said. She glanced across at Belinda, and Belinda shrugged.

'I expect you two are worn out after all this,' said Mr Adams as he opened the front door to Holly's house. 'I think you'd better take yourselves straight up to bed.'

He opened the sitting-room door a crack and closed it again. 'Your mother's still asleep,' he said. 'So you two be quiet. You know what she's like if you disturb her while she's having a nap.'

With feelings of deep frustration the two girls went up to Holly's bedroom. Now what were they to do?

'This is hopeless,' said Holly once she and Belinda were safely in her room. 'I'll just have to risk disturbing her. I'm going to go mad if I don't get a look inside that box pretty soon. Right, you stay up here and I'll go and see if she's woken up. And if she hasn't I'll just try and creep off with the box without waking her.'

'You could always go in there with a cup of coffee, or something for her,' suggested Belinda. 'Then at least you've got a reasonable excuse for waking her.'

'No,' said Holly. 'I'll just creep in there and creep out again. She won't even know the box has gone. I'll be back in thirty seconds at most. You can time me.'

'Shall do,' said Belinda, looking at her watch. 'And if you're not back in one minute I'll send out a search party.'

But it was far more difficult than Holly had thought it would be to get the chocolates away from her mother.

Mrs Adams had settled in front of the television and had the box at her elbow. Her eyes were closed, and for a moment Holly thought she would be able to take the box without being spotted. She hadn't opened it yet, Holly noticed. The bow was still round it.

As Holly reached out her hand, her mother stretched, sighed and opened her eyes.

'Hello, Holly. Back already?' she asked with a suppressed yawn. 'What time is it?'

'Eleven o'clock,' said Holly.

'I must have dozed off.' She sat up and rubbed her eyes. 'How are things at Tracy's house?'

'Not too bad,' said Holly. 'We cleared up as much as we could.' She smiled. 'Not started on your chocolates yet?'

'Chocolates?' Mrs Adams looked down at the box perched on the arm of her chair. 'Oh, yes,' she said. 'I'd almost forgotten about them.' She placed the box on her lap and pulled at the bow. 'Oh, I don't know,' she said. 'I think I'll save them for tomorrow. If I start on them now I'll eat the lot and then I won't be able to sleep.'

'Could I have a look at them?' Holly asked innocently.

'You don't like dark chocolate,' said Mrs Adams.

'I just wanted a look at the box,' said Holly.

'There's nothing on the box,' said her mother.

'No. I know. But . . .' Holly paused, trying to think of an excuse for getting the box out of her mother's hands. 'But Belinda was interested in what sort of centres they have.'

Mrs Adams grinned. 'Oh, I see. Belinda is interested, is she? In that case you'd better take a couple up for her.'

'Can I take the box up?'

'No, you can't,' said Mrs Adams. 'I'm not letting Belinda loose on an entire box of chocolates. You can take a couple.'

'I don't know what sort of centres she likes,' Holly said desperately.

'Then tell her to come down and choose for herself,' said her mother.

'Oh, OK,' said Holly, backing towards the door. 'I'll tell her.'

She ran back upstairs.

'Four and a half minutes,' said Belinda, checking her watch. 'Where are they?'

Holly told her what had happened.

'You're hopeless,' said Belinda. 'And now I suppose I'm going to have to think of something?' She heaved herself up off the bed. 'Belinda to the rescue,' she said, rolling her eyes. 'As usual.'

She went downstairs.

'Hello, Mrs Adams,' she said, smiling brightly.

Mrs Adams gave a laugh and held up the still

unopened box. 'You're welcome to take three or four if you think you'll like them,' she said. 'Although I think you might prefer a couple of milk chocolate biscuits. There's some in the barrel in the kitchen.'

'Actually,' said Belinda, 'I'm not hungry at all.'

Mrs Adams stared at her. 'Are you feeling ill?'

Belinda smiled. 'No,' she said. 'But . . . oh, dear, I suppose I've got to tell you.'

'Tell me what?' Mrs Adams gave her a puzzled look.

'It's about the chocolates,' said Belinda. 'We were hoping to get them away from you without you finding out. It's not Tracy's fault. She didn't realise when she gave them to you, that's all.'

'You're talking in riddles, Belinda,' Mrs Adams said, with a bemused expression on her face. 'What's wrong with them?'

'They belong to Tracy's mum,' Belinda said in a rush. 'It was all a mistake. Tracy found them in the cupboard . . . and . . .' Her voice trailed off.

'Well, why didn't Holly say so?' said Mrs Adams. 'You girls are silly, sometimes.' She handed the box to Belinda.

'I'm sorry,' said Belinda. 'Tracy really did mean to give you a present.'

'There's no need to explain,' said Mrs Adams. 'I don't mind at all. Honestly. And tell Tracy I don't expect presents, anyway.'

Without waiting for Mrs Adams to ask any

awkward questions, Belinda slid out of the room and ran upstairs.

'You got them!' Holly cried in admiration. 'What on earth did you do?'

'Never mind what I did,' said Belinda. 'I got them.' She pushed the box into Holly's hands. 'Open them, then,' she said.

'You're brilliant,' said Holly, pulling at the ribbon.

'I've been telling you that for months,' said Belinda.

Holly drew the ribbon aside and lifted the lid.

There was a slip of crinkly paper on top. Holly lifted it eagerly and turned it over.

'Fascinating,' said Belinda. 'Now we know what's inside all the different shapes.' The top layer of chocolates looked perfectly normal.

'Perhaps Judy wrote something on here in invisible ink?' suggested Holly, holding the slip of paper up to the light.

'Invisible ink?' scoffed Belinda. 'You've got to be joking. The whole idea is that this was the last thing she was able to do before being dragged off by someone. Do you really think she'd have time to go out and get invisible ink?'

'It was just a thought,' said Holly. 'Maybe there's something under this layer?'

'Yes,' Belinda said dryly. 'Another layer.' She picked out a chocolate with an almond on top and bit into it. 'Mmm,' she said. 'Not bad.'

'Belinda! We're not supposed to be eating them.'

'I'm checking that Judy hasn't hidden anything inside them,' said Belinda with a grin. 'Let me try another one.'

'No. Get off,' said Holly. She lifted the whole top layer by its corrugated sheet.

They both peered down at what should have been the second layer. There were no chocolates here. Instead there was something wrapped in tissue paper.

'Suffering cats,' Belinda gasped, staring down into the box. 'There *is* something. I don't believe it.'

Holly carefully picked the wrapped object out of the box. She looked at Belinda.

'What do you think?' she asked.

'Open it,' said Belinda.

'I hope it's not a bomb,' Holly said nervously, holding the tissue-wrapped package across her hands. 'It's quite heavy.'

'Judy's not going to send Tracy a bomb, is she?' Belinda said impatiently. 'Give it to me.' She grabbed the package out of Holly's hands and tore off the tissue. 'You see? It's . . . it's . . . *ohhhh*. Holly, look!'

The light glittered on an ornate necklace in the nest of torn tissue. A beautiful necklace set with diamonds and rubies. A necklace fit for a princess to wear.

The two friends looked at each other in stunned silence, as the fabulous jewels sparkled and shone in Belinda's trembling hands.

5   *A narrow escape*

Holly lifted the sparkling necklace out of Belinda's hands.

'It's fabulous,' she said breathlessly. 'It's absolutely fabulous.' The diamonds and rubies twinkled in their setting of silver filigree as it hung, twisting slowly in Holly's fingers.

For a few moments all the two girls could do was stare in wonder at the beautiful piece of jewellery. It seemed to pull in all the light from Holly's room and throw it dazzlingly out again.

Belinda licked her lips nervously. 'You realise these aren't *real* diamonds, don't you?' she said.

Holly managed to break the spell of the flickering gems to look at Belinda. 'Yes, of course,' she said. 'It must be one of Tracy's uncle's designs. But still . . .' Her voice trailed off.

'It's pretty impressive,' said Belinda. 'I certainly couldn't tell the difference.'

'That's the whole point,' said Holly. 'If it *looked* fake no one would want to wear it.'

'Could I ask a stupid question at this point?' said Belinda. 'What was it doing in the bottom of a box of chocolates, do you suppose?'

Holly looked into the box, hoping to find some note or scribbled message from Judy to help unravel the mystery. There was nothing.

'For safe-keeping?' said Holly. 'Why else?'

'Yes,' Belinda said darkly. 'But safe from whom? And why should Judy send it to Tracy?'

'Tracy!' exclaimed Holly. 'We said we'd phone her as soon as we'd looked in the box.' She rested the necklace gently back into the tissue. 'I'll do it now.'

She met her father on the stairs.

'You're up and about late,' he said. 'Do you know what time it is?'

Holly looked at her watch. It was nearly midnight.

'I was just going to give Tracy a ring,' said Holly. 'To check that everything's all right over there.'

'You won't be very popular ringing at this time of night,' said Mr Adams. 'I'd leave it till the morning if I were you. They're probably both in bed.'

Holly gave him a worried look. 'Yes . . . yes, I suppose so.'

'Come on then,' said her father. 'Up to bed. I've locked up and turned all the lights out.' He led her back upstairs, his arm around her shoulders. 'And make sure you get some sleep, you two,' he said with a smile. 'No sitting up all night listening for burglars. OK?'

Holly nodded, said goodnight, and went back into her room.

'No go,' she said to Belinda. 'It's too late to phone her now. What are you up to?'

Belinda was standing at the mirror, holding the necklace against herself. 'Nothing,' she said. She gave a shamefaced laugh. 'Well, all right, I was seeing how it might look on me, that's all.'

'It'd look better without that tatty sweat-shirt of yours,' said Holly. 'You'd need to have something extremely posh to go with a necklace like that.'

'I've got posh clothes,' said Belinda. 'My wardrobe's full of posh clothes. I just never wear any of them. My mother buys them, I try them on once to keep her happy, and then,' she gave a big grin, 'I stuff them out of sight and forget about them.'

Holly hung the necklace over the mirror and the two girls got ready for bed.

They lay in bed, looking at the necklace as it glimmered in the soft light of Holly's bedside lamp.

'Remember Tracy telling us about the new collection her uncle was putting together?' said Holly. 'The ones based on the Thai royal jewellery? Do you suppose this could be one of them? It looks good enough for royalty.'

'It could be,' Belinda said sleepily. 'How much is costume jewellery worth?'

'I don't know. If it was real it would be worth a small fortune.'

Belinda giggled. 'I was just thinking,' she said. 'I was just imagining my mother's face if I appeared at her charity party wearing it.'

'You'd better not,' said Holly. 'If this is one of Scheherazade's new designs, then it's still top secret. Remember what Tracy said? All their new designs are kept secret, in case rival companies steal them and sell them as their own.'

Belinda sat up. 'Do you think that's it?' she said. 'Do you think this really could be a brand new design that no one's supposed to see?' She looked eagerly at Holly. 'That would explain why Judy sent it to Tracy hidden in a chocolate box.'

'Would it?' said Holly. 'I don't see why.'

'Well,' began Belinda. 'Just imagine. Judy and . . . what's his name? That man who came over with her?'

'Tony Meyer.'

'Yes, him. Judy and Tony Meyer come to London. We know Tony Meyer was over here on business. So, if he's trying to sell Scheherazade's new designs, he'd bring a sample, wouldn't he?'

'I'm with you so far,' said Holly.

'OK,' said Belinda, her eyes gleaming. 'What if there was a spy, or something, from a rival firm? Someone else on the aeroplane with them? Waiting for them to get to London. Waiting for the chance to grab the new design off them?'

'And Judy and Tony Meyer realised what was going on,' finished Holly. 'But only had a short

58

time to get the necklace away somewhere out of reach.'

'That's it!' said Belinda, bouncing excitedly on the bed. 'They had just enough time to hide the necklace and send it off to Tracy before they were grabbed by these rivals. And they were held hostage until they admitted what they'd done with it.'

'No, no,' said Holly. 'What about the phone call?'

'It was a fake,' said Belinda. 'Just like Tracy said all along. They were already being held hostage when they made the call. Judy probably told them she was expected up here, so they got her to make the phone call so we wouldn't be suspicious when she didn't arrive.'

Holly stared in horror at her friend. 'And they ransacked Tracy's house, looking for the parcel – just as we thought.'

'But it wasn't there,' said Belinda. 'Because Tracy had already brought it over here. Without realising what it was. It all fits.'

'Yes, yes, of *course* it does,' said Holly. 'Tracy told us her uncle was having problems with people stealing his designs. That *must* be what this is all about.' She let out a long breath, gazing across at the glittering necklace. 'And we've got it.' She gave Belinda an uneasy look. 'It's a good thing no one *knows* we've got it,' she said. 'What should we do?'

59

'Hide it,' said Belinda. 'And then, first thing tomorrow, we go and pick Tracy up and go to the police.'

There was a rap on the door. 'Aren't you two girls asleep yet?' called Mrs Adams. 'It's gone twelve, you know.'

'It's OK,' shouted Holly. 'We're just turning the light off.'

They lay quietly in the darkness, listening to the sound of Mrs Adams's feet in the hall and the click as Holly's parents' bedroom door closed.

'Where can we hide it?' whispered Holly. 'If these people are already in Willow Dale, it won't take them long to find out we're Tracy's friends. Then all they've got to do is put two and two together.'

'I've got an idea,' whispered Belinda. 'My dad's got a wall safe. We can put it there tomorrow. That'll be as secure as anywhere until we get to the police.'

'OK, then,' whispered Holly. '*First* thing in the morning. I don't want that thing in the house a moment longer than necessary.'

After Tracy had waved goodnight to her friends, she turned and saw her mother standing in the kitchen doorway. Mrs Foster looked tired out.

'Shall we go to bed?' said Tracy. 'There's not much more we can do now.' She smiled wanly. 'I'm wiped out,' she said with a sigh. 'And you look beat, too.'

'I don't know that I'll be able to sleep, honey,' said Mrs Foster. 'This thing has got me so wound up I don't think I could even close my eyes.'

'I know,' said Tracy. 'What we need is a milky drink. That'll help us both sleep.'

She linked arms with her mother and they walked into the kitchen together.

'You just sit there,' said Tracy gently. 'I'll make it.'

Mrs Foster had got the kitchen almost back to normal. The burglars had concentrated their worst efforts in other parts of the house.

'You're a good girl, Tracy,' said Mrs Foster.

'I am, aren't I?' said Tracy with a smile. 'And you're a good mom.' She opened the fridge. 'Oh, great,' she said. 'We're out of milk. Brilliant.'

'Never mind,' said Mrs Foster. 'It was a nice idea.'

'It still *is* a nice idea,' said Tracy. 'You wait here. I'll only be five minutes.'

'Where are you going?'

'There's that corner shop,' said Tracy, pulling her anorak on. 'They're open all hours. I'll just run down there and get some milk.'

Mrs Foster was too tired to argue with her. 'Be careful,' she said.

'I'll be back before you know it,' said Tracy.

The street lights shone pools of light on to the damp pavement. The corner shop was only a short jog away, but Tracy couldn't help noticing the way shadows seemed to lurk menacingly under normally friendly trees. Bushes in front gardens took on alarming shapes and the gloom of doorways seemed to glitter with sinister eyes.

'Pull yourself together,' Tracy told herself.

But it was all so terribly quiet.

The air was cold and Tracy shivered as she ran back from the shop with the carton of milk. Hunched into her jacket, her thoughts still on the burglary, she didn't notice a car, its headlights darkened, driving slowly down the street. Suddenly, the car accelerated, swerved to the side of the road and mounted the pavement right beside her.

The rear door crashed open and a hand reached out and grabbed Tracy's arm. She felt sharp fingers digging into the flesh under her anorak. The hand slipped, clutched again, and began to pull her towards the car.

Tracy felt her feet slide. She was losing her balance. The inside of the car was dark, and although she could see that the hand holding her was a man's, she could see nothing else of him in the gloom.

Fear gave Tracy a spurt of strength.

She twisted her body and dodged away from the grasping hand. From the driver's seat a harsh male voice snarled with a distinctive American accent, 'Don't let her get away, you fool!'

'Shut up!' An English voice. A deep angry voice from the back of the car. The hand that held her was thin and wired with veins. 'Help me, I can't hold her.'

The clutching fingers were slipping on the shiny material of Tracy's anorak.

A second hand snaked out of the darkened interior of the car. Tracy saw the glimmer of rings in the light of the street lamp. She knew she wouldn't be strong enough to escape if the driver of the car got hold of her as well. This was her last chance.

She kicked out at the thin hand, the toe of her shoe striking hard under the wrist. There was a cry of pain and the fingers relaxed for an instant.

That was all Tracy needed. She wrenched her arm free and ran.

It was only a short distance to the corner of her own street, but it seemed like miles.

Making a sudden decision, Tracy ducked into an alleyway and ran full pelt. They wouldn't be able to get the car down there. They would have to follow her on foot.

She was about to scale a low wall when she heard the screech of the car at the mouth of the alley.

Her heart thundered in her chest, but instead of the dreaded sound of pursuit, she heard the engine rev and fade.

She took in a few deep breaths, controlling

herself. Listening intently. Ready to dive into cover.

But there was nothing. No sound at all.

Had they gone? Or was one of them lurking at the end of the alley, waiting for her to emerge? As cautiously as a cat, Tracy crept towards the street.

Was that someone in the shadows? No. Just a trailing rose bush making eerie patterns in the night.

With a gasp of relief, Tracy came out on to the pavement. They had gone.

Whoever they had been, whatever they had wanted, they had gone.

Tracy ran home.

She closed the front door.

'Mom?'

There was no answer. A new panic hit her. Clutching the carton of milk, she ran into the kitchen.

Her mother's head was in her arms on the table. Tracy let out a gasp of relief.

Mrs Foster had finally succumbed to the exertions of the day and had fallen asleep where she sat.

Tracy shook her gently. 'Mom?'

Mrs Foster awoke with a start. 'Oh! Tracy!' She rubbed her arm across her eyes. 'It looks like I shan't be needing that milk after all,' she said. 'I'm dead on my feet.'

Tracy looked sympathetically at her. There didn't seem any need to tell her what had happened right then. She could tell her in the morning. That would be soon enough.

Mrs Foster stood up. 'I'll just check everything is locked up,' she said.

'No, you won't,' Tracy said firmly. 'You go to bed. Leave all that to me.'

Mrs Foster nodded wearily and went upstairs.

Tracy went around the house, checking that all the windows were properly fastened and the lower ones locked with their security bolts. The doors were all locked and bolted. There was no way that an intruder could possibly get in.

She lay in bed a few minutes later, wondering about the men in the car. There were two of them, one to drive and the other to grab Tracy. She shut her eyes, trying to bring back to her memory exactly what had happened. Two men. An American in the driving seat, and an Englishman in the back.

What was it they wanted? To pull her off the street and . . . and *what*? *Kidnap* her? The idea was bizarre. Mrs Foster had no money. Neither Tracy nor her mother could possibly have anything of value.

Or did they? The parcel. The parcel from Judy.

Tracy's mind spun in the darkness. Of course! Her friends had already guessed that the burglary was something to do with Judy's curious parcel. In

Tracy's mind, this attempt to grab her off the street only went to confirm that.

They wanted that package. They wanted it desperately enough to risk abducting her to get it.

And even more frightening to Tracy was the thought that if they were prepared to do *that*, what had they already done to Judy?

They knew the package had been sent to Tracy. And they could only know that if they already *had* Judy.

'I was right,' Tracy murmured to herself. 'I was right about Judy all the time, and no one believed me.'

She sat up in bed. They'd have to believe her now. Someone would believe her. Uncle Jason would believe her.

Tracy frowned with frustration. Uncle Jason and Aunt Merrilyn would be somewhere in the Catskill Mountains by now. Out of contact.

But there was that phone number that Tony Meyer had given her. If she could get a message to New York – a message letting Uncle Jason know Judy was in danger – he'd be sure to do something.

Tracy snapped on her bedside light and groped for her watch. How did the time zones work between the UK and America? New York time was four, no, five hours behind English time. So if it was midnight here – she checked her watch: half

66

past midnight already! Half past midnight here, then it must be seven thirty in the evening in New York.

She didn't know whether the number was an office or a private one. But surely someone must be there most of the time: there was no point giving people an emergency number if you couldn't speak to someone pretty quickly.

Tiptoeing downstairs so that she didn't wake her mother, Tracy slid into the small back room her mother used as an office and picked up the phone. The curtains were still pulled back and the faint glow from outside gave just enough light for her to be able to find the number and to dial.

She listened to the soft purr down the lines. If it was an office number she might only get an answering machine. She tried to think what sort of message she should leave. 'This is Tracy Foster calling from England. Please ring back immediately.'

She gave a gasp of relief as the purring stopped and a voice spoke.

'Hello?' Tracy gripped the receiver tightly, welcoming the American accent of the man who had picked up the phone.

'I need to speak to Jason Stern,' said Tracy. 'It's very urgent.'

'I'm afraid Mr Stern is on vacation right now. Who am I speaking to, please?'

'My name's Tracy Foster. I'm calling from

England. I'm Mr Stern's niece.'

'Uh-huh?' said the voice unconcernedly. 'Please give me your message and I'll do my best to get it to Mr Stern.'

'It's about his daughter,' said Tracy. 'She's supposed to be staying with me, but something's happened to her.' Her voice speeded up as she poured out the whole story down the phone, including the burglary and the men in the car. 'And I'm sure Judy is in some really bad danger,' she said. 'Tell my uncle I'll be contacting the police here.'

'I think you should wait for your uncle to get in touch before you do anything like that,' said the voice smoothly. 'You're going to look kind of silly if Miss Stern has simply stayed in London for a couple of days.'

Tracy stared at the phone. Had he been *listening*? Had he been paying any attention at all?

'I *know* something's wrong,' she said.

'I don't think so,' said the voice. 'You see, I've only just been speaking to Mr Meyer on the phone, not two hours ago, and he told me they were seeing the sights.'

'You've spoken to him?' gasped Tracy. 'You know where they are?'

'Sure. They're staying at a hotel. You see? There's nothing for you to worry about.'

'Which hotel?' asked Tracy.

'I'm sorry. He didn't tell me that. Look, Miss

Foster, I'll see what I can do about contacting Mr Stern. Your best bet is to wait until he rings you.'

There was something wrong about this. It simply didn't tie in with what had been happening recently.

'OK,' she said, as calmly as she could. 'But there's just one thing you might be able to help me with. Judy told me her dog, Harry, was ill. Can you tell me if he's any better, please?'

'Oh, yes, Harry? Yes, he's just fine. No problem.'

Tracy put the phone down.

She looked at the pad where she had scribbled the number. The emergency phone number that she had been given by the man pretending to be Tony Meyer. It was a fake. Judy no more had a sick dog called Harry than Tracy did. The whole thing had been set up to fool them. Judy *was* in danger. And the danger had come from America with her.

But what could she do now?

'Think, Tracy, *think*,' she said to herself.

A gleam of light caught her eye through the window. A moving chink of light out at the back of the house.

A torch? It flickered, wavered and went out. A few seconds later it was snapped on again.

Any other night Tracy might have assumed it was a neighbour, out looking for a lost cat. But any other night she would have been asleep in bed, not walking round the house after a burglary and an attempted abduction. And neighbours

69

wouldn't be out looking for their cats at a quarter to one in the morning.

Her skin prickled. There was something sinister about this. The torchlight was moving closer.

She slipped behind the heavy velvet curtain, keeping out of sight. She was just in time. The torchlight played around the room, then moved away again.

Tracy hardly dared breathe. Cautiously, an inch at a time, she moved her head to see where the light had gone.

Then she saw him. Someone in dark trousers, silhouetted against the faint lights of the flats beyond the terrace gardens. He was peering upwards.

At Tracy's bedroom window.

She could see the dark wall of the kitchen, and its little strip of garden against the lower wall which divided the two houses. She could see the pitch of the kitchen roof, lower than the rest of the house, with a drainpipe at the corner.

And she could see the figure test the drainpipe, change his mind, move a plastic dustbin to the corner and begin to climb up on to the roof which went up to Tracy's bedroom window.

6 Night-time intruder

Tracy backed behind the curtain again and stealthily reached out her hand for the telephone, feeling for the buttons, fingering the one for calling 999.

Suddenly a light blazed above her from her mother's room, highlighting the intruder, who slipped from the dustbin and melted away into the darkness.

In the distance Tracy heard a car start up and drive away.

She dropped her hand from the phone and pulled the curtains across before snapping on the desk light.

'Tracy?'

The hall light was now on, and her mother, tousle-headed, stood in the doorway. 'What are you doing? You frightened the life out of me.'

'I – I was just about to call the police,' said Tracy, annoyed to find her voice shaking. 'I couldn't sleep, so I came down for a drink.' She didn't want to tell her mother about the call to New York, not until she had got a few more things clear in her head. 'There was a light – in the garden. A torch.'

'Tracy, honey, you've had a shock with the burglary this evening. It was probably just a reflection or something.'

'No,' said Tracy. 'It was a man.' She opened the curtain again. 'Look – he moved the dustbin,' she said. 'He was going to climb up to my room.'

The light from the hall and the back room shone down the little garden area to the dustbin standing out of place at the corner of the house.

Mrs Foster paled. 'We'd better call the police right away,' she said. She lifted the receiver and dialled, just as Tracy had been about to do a few moments ago. She spoke briskly into the mouthpiece.

'I heard a noise in the house,' Mrs Foster explained to Tracy after she had put the receiver down. 'It woke me up.'

'That was probably me,' said Tracy. 'I was trying to be quiet.'

'I came down to investigate.' Mrs Foster gave a grim smile. 'I was looking around for a weapon of some sort. It was a good thing you were about, Tracy. We managed to frighten him off.' She gave Tracy a puzzled look. 'Could it possibly be the same burglar back again? Might he have seen something earlier and . . . no, no. That can't be right, surely. We've nothing of value here.'

Tracy couldn't keep it to herself any longer. 'I think he was trying to kidnap me!' she blurted out.

'Kidnap you? Tracy, what on earth makes you think that?'

'Because they've already tried once before,' Tracy explained in a rush. 'When I went out. Two men came along in a car and tried to drag me into it.' She shivered at the memory.

'Tracy! Why didn't you tell me about this?' Mrs Foster clutched at her daughter as if to protect her. 'This evening, you mean? When you went out for the milk? I *knew* I shouldn't have let you go.'

'You looked so tired,' said Tracy. 'And I've been out at night lots of times. I'm all right really. They didn't get me.'

'But supposing they had!' Mrs Foster cried. 'You should have told me straightaway, Tracy.'

'Like I said, I didn't want you to have anything else to worry about,' said Tracy. 'I thought it could wait till the morning.'

'Well, it's morning now, though a bit early,' Mrs Foster said. 'Now, then. Tell me exactly what happened.'

As they waited for the police to arrive, blinking with tiredness and shivering in their dressing-gowns, Tracy told her mother about the car in the road, and about the suspicions that the girls had over the parcel from her cousin.

'It's something to do with Judy,' said Tracy. 'Something's happened to her. I know it has.'

Mrs Foster looked uneasily at her. 'You should have told me this before,' she said.

'I did try,' said Tracy. 'But you didn't believe me.'

'And this parcel – the chocolates from Judy – where are they now?'

'Holly's mom has them,' said Tracy.

Mrs Foster looked solemnly at her. 'We'd better tell the police everything when they arrive,' she said. She smiled tiredly and put her arm around Tracy.

'Don't worry,' she said. 'They'll find her.'

'I hope so,' said Tracy. 'I really hope so.'

The police officers nodded grimly as Tracy told them everything she suspected.

It was a relief for her finally to be able to give voice to her worries to someone who actually listened and seemed to take her seriously.

While one of the police officers wrote down all she said, the other was out sweeping the garden with a torch.

'I think I've spotted a few footprints round by the dustbin,' he said, coming back in the house. 'We'll send someone round to take some casts in the morning.'

The other officer was looking at his notes. 'Could you say if the man you saw in the garden was the same one from the car?' he asked.

'I really don't know,' said Tracy. 'It was all so *quick*.'

'Could you describe the clothes they were

wearing?' asked the policeman gently.

Tracy looked anxiously at him, shaking her head. She had always prided herself on her powers of observation. She had always thought of herself as *exactly* the right person to be a witness at a crime. And now she found she could remember nothing of the men. It could have been the same man – or two completely different men. It was *so* frustrating.

'I'm sorry,' said Tracy. 'I didn't get much of a look at either of them.' Her mother put an arm protectively around her.

'Not to worry,' said the policeman. 'You're tired. You might well find that you'll remember a lot more in the morning. After a good night's sleep.' He closed his notebook. 'You've already given us a lot of good information. The first thing we'll have to do is check down in London. See if we can't trace your cousin's movements once she got off the plane.' He stood up, nodding to his colleague. 'What I'd like you both to do now is get some sleep, if you can. They won't be back tonight, you can be sure of that. And I'll make sure someone is keeping an extra eye on this street.'

'You'll try and contact Judy's parents in America?' asked Mrs Foster.

The police officer nodded. 'We'll do that, for sure,' he said. He looked at Tracy. 'Now,' he said, 'I'd like you and your mother to come down to the station first thing in the morning. And you'd better bring that package you told us about.'

'You've got to find Judy,' said Tracy.

'We will,' said the police officer. 'Don't you worry.'

As Mrs Foster closed the front door after the departing police officers, they heard the sounds of the dawn chorus piping up in the darkness.

'Will you be able to sleep?' asked Mrs Foster.

'I think so,' said Tracy. 'I'm dead tired.'

Her mother nodded. 'Me, too,' she said.

Tracy pulled her bedcovers up over her ears. At last the long, anxious night was over and she could try to get some rest.

Tracy was woken by the telephone bell urgently shrilling downstairs in the hall. It was ten o'clock in the morning.

Bleary-eyed she went to answer the phone.

Holly's excited voice came over the wire. 'Tracy, you'll never believe what we found in your chocolate box!'

Tracy rubbed the sleep out of her eyes. 'And you won't believe what's been happening to me,' she said. 'Oh . . . I can't *tell* you. We've had the police round, and everything. I've told them all about Judy.' Tracy was suddenly alert. 'Have you still got the box, Holly?'

'Yes. It's safe. I'm at Belinda's house. But, Tracy . . . there was a necklace in it. A beautiful diamond and ruby necklace.'

76

'A necklace?' gasped Tracy.

'Yes. Belinda – shut up – I'm *telling* her. We think it's one of your uncle's new designs. It's absolutely fabulous.'

'I'll come right over,' said Tracy. 'Stay there.'

Tracy ran up to her mother's bedroom. She knocked and opened the door.

'Mom? Are you awake?' She tiptoed towards the bed. She could hear the deep, rhythmic sound of her mother's breathing.

'Mom?' There was no response from the slumbering figure in the bed.

'OK, Mom,' said Tracy softly. 'You sleep. We'll deal with this.'

She crept out of the house and made her way over to where Belinda lived.

'You look like you've only just crawled out of bed,' said Belinda, opening the door to her. 'You look terrible.'

'I've been up most of the night,' said Tracy. 'Didn't Holly tell you?'

Belinda led her into the kitchen, where Holly was waiting. The two girls listened in stunned silence as Tracy told them the full story of what had happened to her the previous night.

'It must have been the same men,' exclaimed Holly. 'They've got Judy and Tony Meyer, and now they want the necklace.' She let out a breath. 'Well, they won't get it now. It's in Belinda's father's safe.'

77

'All this for fake jewellery,' breathed Belinda. 'What would they do if they were real?'

'Don't even think about it,' said Tracy.

'It seems a shame just to have to hand everything over to the police, though,' said Holly. 'After everything we've been through.'

'Everything *I've* been through, you mean,' said Tracy. 'I'm the one that nearly got kidnapped last night.'

'Exactly,' said Holly. 'So you're the only one who knows what these men look like.'

'I told you,' wailed Tracy. 'I *don't* know what they look like at all.'

'You must have some idea,' said Belinda. 'For instance, the car. What was the car like?'

'I don't remember. A four door saloon of some sort,' said Tracy.

'I know,' said Belinda. 'You need something hot and sweet to drink. That'll help get your brain working. I'll make some hot chocolate, shall I? You should always drink something hot and sweet after a shock.'

'I'm not shocked,' said Tracy. 'I'm just exhausted.'

Belinda shrugged. 'I'll make some anyway. Just in case.' She grinned at Tracy. 'You sit down and I'll rustle up some breakfast.'

'I'm not really hungry,' said Tracy.

'I am,' said Belinda. 'I haven't eaten for hours.'

The three friends went over Tracy's story again.

Holly tried her best to jog Tracy's memory, but it was no good. Apart from the fact that one of the men in the car was an American and the other was English, she couldn't remember anything.

'At least we know what they were after,' said Holly. 'They wanted to get their hands on that necklace.'

'Could I see it?' asked Tracy.

Belinda went into another room.

She came back a few moments later. Tracy leaned forward as Belinda carefully unwrapped the parcel. As she held the jewellery up the diamonds and rubies glittered in the morning light of the Hayes' kitchen.

'Wow!' breathed Tracy. 'It looks so real, doesn't it? No wonder my uncle's rivals want to get it. It explains why Scheherazade's designs are so sought after.'

'I'm glad it's not real,' said Holly. 'It would be worth thousands of pounds.'

'Hundreds of thousands,' added Tracy. 'Maybe even millions.'

'It all ties in now,' said Belinda. 'This must be one of your uncle's new designs. The ones he's basing on that Thai royal jewellery. Someone is obviously desperate to get their hands on it.'

'Desperate enough to ransack your house,' Holly said to Tracy. 'And to try and grab you off the street. The question is, why?'

'Don't you see?' said Tracy. 'It's a brand new

design. If someone, some rival jeweller, got their hands on it, they could make copies. They could sell it as their own design. Was there anything else in the box? Any message from Judy?'

'We tore it to bits,' said Belinda. 'There wasn't anything. I even cut all the chocolates in half before I ate them, to see if there were secret messages hidden inside.'

'The man who tried to grab you was the same one who's got Judy,' said Holly. 'And the same one who telephoned pretending to be Tony Meyer.'

'Unless,' Tracy began hesitantly. 'Unless it *was* Tony Meyer. Perhaps it was him all along. Who better to know about the new designs? If Judy somehow realised what was going on she could have had time to get the necklace from him. It makes sense. My uncle was sure the new designs were being sold by someone in his own company. Judy told me that. And Tony Meyer is his right-hand man.'

'We've got to try to fit a few more clues together,' said Holly. 'Try to remember the car, Tracy. What colour was it?'

'It was a dark colour,' said Tracy. 'I remember that much.'

'What about inside?' asked Belinda.

Holly had taken out the Mystery Club's notebook and was scribbling things down.

'Did a light come on when they opened the door?' she asked.

'No. I don't think so,' said Tracy.

'This is hopeless,' said Belinda.

'No, wait!' said Tracy. 'I'm trying to picture it in my mind.' Tracy looked at them. 'I *must* have seen the colour,' she said. 'if only I could – wait! Wait. Yes! It was green. Very dark green.' She flopped back in her chair. 'And the upholstery was green as well.'

'There you are,' said Holly. 'I knew you'd remember if you tried.' She wrote this down in the notebook. 'Just a minute,' she said. 'Don't you remember that car outside your house yesterday? Wasn't that green? And it had green upholstery too.'

'I don't know,' said Tracy. 'I didn't really see it. I was too busy worrying about the burglary.'

'I'll bet you it was the same car,' said Holly, rereading what she had written.

Belinda handed Tracy a mug of hot chocolate. 'Drink that,' she said. 'And keep thinking.'

Tracy took a sip. 'Belinda! How much sugar have you put in this?'

'Only my usual three spoonfuls,' said Belinda. 'It's good for your brain.'

'The man in the front of the car had rings on three of his fingers,' said Tracy.

'See? What did I tell you about sugar?' said Belinda. 'You'll be able to tell us his name next.'

'Hardly,' said Tracy. 'But it's something, isn't it? Something else we can tell the police.'

'And we know he isn't working alone,' said Belinda. 'We know there's an Englishman involved. What was his accent like?'

'Oh, local,' said Tracy. 'It was a normal Yorkshire accent, like everyone around here.'

'So we know he's working with a local man,' said Holly. 'OK, so what sort of person would be likely to get involved with something like this?'

'A criminal?' suggested Belinda.

'Very helpful,' said Holly. 'No. I mean, what sort of *criminal* would be likely to want to help someone who's involved in selling the designs of costume jewellery? Don't you see what I'm getting at? It wouldn't be someone who wanted the necklace itself. It would have to be someone who was interested in getting hold of the *design*.'

'*Ohhh . . .*' gasped Belinda. 'You mean another jeweller?'

Holly gave a triumphant grin. 'Exactly.'

'Well,' said Belinda. 'There's half a dozen jewellers' shops in Willow Dale alone. And there must be hundreds within easy driving distance.'

'Driving distance?' repeated Holly. 'That's another point. If Tony Meyer is behind all this, where has he got a car from? He can't have brought it over on the aeroplane.'

'He must have hired one,' said Tracy.

'Just a minute,' said Holly. 'There was a sticker of some sort in the back of that car I saw outside your house last night.' She went through her notes. 'Yes! here it is. A checkered sticker in the back window.'

'You never said anything about that,' said Tracy. 'I can tell you what that is. My mom uses them sometimes. It's a local firm. They're just called Checkered Car Hire.'

'Belinda,' Holly cried excitedly. 'Get the phone book. We've got the number plate and the colour. If we phone them they might tell us who hired the car.' She grinned at her friends. 'At this rate we'll have the whole thing solved before we even *go* to the police!'

It was easy enough for them to find the phone number of Checkered Car Hire. Belinda and Tracy sat eagerly listening as Holly dialled.

The woman at the other end of the phone was polite and reasonable when Holly asked after the green car.

'Yes,' she said. 'It sounds like one of ours.'

Holly did a thumbs-up to her friends. Another few seconds and they'd know for certain whether it was Tony Meyer who had hired the car. That would be a real scoop to take to the police.

'I'd need to look up the files to check the number plate,' continued the woman. 'Could you tell me why you're enquiring? Has there been an accident?'

'Oh, no,' said Holly. 'Nothing like that. I'd just

like to know the name of the person who hired it, please.'

The voice changed down the phone, becoming more businesslike. 'We don't give out information like that,' she said.

'But it's really important,' Holly said desperately.

'I'm very sorry,' said the woman.

Holly put the phone down and the three girls looked at one another.

'Rats!' said Tracy. 'I knew that was too easy to be true.' She looked at her watch. 'I'd better get off to the police station now. They'll be wondering what's happened to me.'

'Are we taking this?' asked Belinda, holding up the necklace.

'I'd rather not,' said Tracy. 'Just in case we're followed.' She gave her friends an emphatic look. 'They seem to have a pretty good idea of our movements. I don't want to risk it.'

'I'll put it back in the safe, then,' said Belinda. 'The police can always pop round if they want to have a look at it.'

'I hope they're not going to dust it for fingerprints,' said Holly. 'They'll find more of ours than anyone else's.' She sighed. 'Some investigators we are. Why didn't we think of that before we started handling it?'

They put the necklace into the wall safe and were about to leave when the phone rang.

Holly and Tracy waited in the hall while Belinda answered the phone.

She came out looking gloomy. 'That was my mother,' she said. 'Apparently she's expecting a delivery of some stuff for the party tonight. She wants me to stay in and wait for it.' She sighed heavily. 'Looks like you'll have to go without me.' She sat on the stairs with her chin on her fists. 'I never get to do anything interesting around here. I hate her parties.'

'They do make a lot of money for charities,' Holly reminded her.

'And Judy was going to give a talk at this one,' said Tracy sadly. 'Lordy, I *wish* she was here to do it.'

Holly looked sympathetically at Belinda. 'I could stay and keep you company, if you like?' she suggested. 'Tracy can tell the police everything.'

'Of course I can,' said Tracy. 'You two stay here.' She grinned. 'You can guard the necklace.' She opened the front door. 'I'll meet you later in town, if you like.'

'That's a good idea,' said Holly. 'We wanted to get Belinda some make-up for tonight anyway.' She smiled at Belinda. 'For your starring role at the party.'

'*Don't*,' moaned Belinda. 'It's bad enough without you two making fun. You are both still coming, aren't you? You're not just going to leave me to it?'

'I think I'd rather take a raincheck on it,' said

Tracy. 'I want to be at home this evening. In case there's any news. And I don't want to leave my mom on her own.'

'Of course you don't,' said Belinda. 'Don't worry about it. Holly will be here to keep me company.'

'I'll do my best,' said Holly. She looked round at Tracy. 'Where shall we meet?'

'Oh, how's about Annie's Tea-room – at about half past two? I'll wait around for you in case you're late. But don't leave it too long, I want to get home as soon as I can.'

They said goodbye to Tracy and settled down to wait for the delivery for Mrs Hayes' party.

'I've been thinking,' said Belinda, a couple of hours later, coming into the sitting-room with a plate of sandwiches for the two of them.

'What about, need I ask?' said Holly. In between bouts of watching daytime television and waiting for the delivery men, both girls had had time to do a lot of thinking about Judy and the necklace.

'Oh, you know,' said Belinda, sitting down and putting the plate on the sofa between them. 'Just trying to get it all clear in my head. What do you think has actually happened to Judy?'

'If we're right about Tony Meyer being behind it all, then he's obviously got her locked up some-where,' said Holly. 'I suppose he'll keep hold of her until he gets his hands on the necklace.'

'Yes,' said Belinda. 'That's what's puzzling me.

Where do you suppose she sent the necklace from?'

'London,' said Holly. 'Except that we couldn't read the postmark.'

'If she sent it from London,' Belinda said thoughtfully, 'then he must have her locked up in London. Wouldn't you say?'

'I suppose so.'

'So how come he's up here? Miles away? He wouldn't *leave* her somewhere would he? He'd want her somewhere close at hand so he could keep an eye on her.'

'I see what you're getting at,' said Holly. 'If Meyer and his accomplice are *here*, actually in Willow Dale, then maybe Judy is somewhere nearby as well.' Holly nodded thoughtfully at this new idea. 'That's terrible, isn't it? To think she might be only a few miles away, locked up somewhere, and we can't do a thing to help her.'

'Can't we, though?' said Belinda, a dark grin spreading over her face. 'I've had an idea how my mother's horrible party might come in useful for once. If the police don't come round to pick up that necklace before tonight, I think there's something we could try.'

'I'd try anything,' Holly said eagerly, 'if it meant we could solve this before the police do.' She frowned. 'Well, *almost* anything. What have you got in mind?'

'You know the sort of people my mother has

invited round tonight, don't you?' said Belinda. 'I've seen the invitation list. Just about every major business person for miles around is coming.' She grinned. 'You know my mother and her social contacts.'

'So?' said Holly, unable to follow her friend's train of thought.

'The house will be stacked out with company directors and factory owners, and with the managers of all the big local shops. She always gets them to come along. All the shops from the town centre. The big ones, anyway.' Belinda laughed at the look of incomprehension on Holly's face. 'You still don't get it, do you? What were we talking about earlier? About the sort of person who'd be interested in stealing Scheherazade's new designs?'

'Jewellers!' exclaimed Holly.

'Got it in one,' said Belinda. 'There's guaranteed to be a few of them around. Maybe even the very person we're looking for.' Belinda waved a sandwich at Holly. 'Now, how do you think such a person would react if they actually *saw* the new Scheherazade design adorning someone's neck?'

'They'd have a heart attack, I expect,' said Holly.

'Well, maybe not quite a heart attack,' Belinda said with a laugh. 'But there'd certainly be *some* reaction, wouldn't you say?'

Holly gazed open-mouthed at her. 'That's brilliant,' she said. 'We could be watching to see if anyone does a double-take when they see it. And if anyone does – bang! – we've got them.' She frowned. 'There's only one problem, though. Who's going to wear it?'

Belinda folded her arms and gave Holly a wonderfully haughty, superior look down her nose.

'Who's got a wardrobe full of dresses to go with it?' she said. 'Who's the most aristocratic person you can think of?'

Holly burst out laughing. 'You?'

'Yes, why not me?' said Belinda.

Holly was about to open her mouth to reply when they heard the crunch of tyres in the gravel drive.

A few moments later there was a loud ring at the doorbell and the two friends went to tell the delivery men where to put the boxes.

Ten minutes later they were heading into town, eager to hear from Tracy what had happened at the police station, and eager to tell her Belinda's plan.

They had no way of knowing that Tracy had never even got to the police station.

7 The American man

Tracy still felt sleepy as she sat on the bus taking
her to the town centre. She smiled to herself,
thinking that if it had been Belinda who had been
up all night being grabbed at from cars and scaring
off would-be kidnappers, she'd have had to sleep
for a couple of days solid to get over it.

But even someone as fit and healthy as Tracy
couldn't expect to be on top form after only a few
hours' sleep. And here she was, almost nodding
off on the bus.

She opened a window and took a few deep
breaths to clear her head. She'd need to have all
her wits about her once she arrived at the police
station.

She got off the bus in the centre of Willow Dale,
enjoying the gentle breeze as she crossed the road.
There were plenty of people about. She looked at
her watch. Hardly surprising, really; it was already
early afternoon.

'Excuse me.' She turned at the voice. It was a tall,
thin-faced man with blond curly hair. He had a
collection of camera stuff hanging round his neck

and was wearing sunglasses.

He smiled. 'Could you help me out, please?' He had a folded map in his hands.

It was quite a surprise to hear an American accent. Not that Willow Dale wasn't often full of tourists in the summer, but it was less usual at this time of year.

'I can try,' said Tracy. 'What's the problem?'

The man's smile broadened. 'Hey, you're American, aren't you?' he said.

Tracy laughed. 'I thought I'd lost most of my accent,' she said. 'I've lived in England for three years now.'

'You don't say?' The man shook his head. 'But I can always tell a fellow countryman,' he said with a laugh. 'Country *girl*, I should say.' He waved the map. 'I've kind of gotten myself lost. I'm terrible with maps. My wife's always telling me so. She says I'm the only man she knows who could get lost between the dining-room and the kitchen.'

He's funny, thought Tracy. *But he's a bit silly.*

'Where do you want to be?' asked Tracy.

The man turned and lowered the folded map so that she could see where he was pointing.

'Woodfree Abbey,' he said. 'I'm supposed to meet my wife and kids there, but I'm darned if I can figure it out.'

'Oh, that's easy,' Tracy said with a smile. She knew the Abbey well. She ought to; the first adventure the Mystery Club had ever been

91

involved in had centred around Woodfree Abbey.

But suddenly Tracy's smile faded. The man had a deep tan. On his face and on the backs of his hands. The sort of deep, American tan that Tracy still regretted having lost.

But across the base of three of his fingers the skin was much whiter. There were three pale hoops where the sun had not been able to darken his skin.

Her mind flashed back to the previous night. The car pulling up. The hand reaching out to grab her arm. Struggling to get free. A second hand – from the driver of the car. A hand with three rings on the clawing fingers.

The man smiled. 'Easy for you, maybe,' he said. 'But not so easy for poor Joe Schmo here.'

Tracy tried to maintain her smile, although every instinct in her was screaming for her to yell and run. Was it really the man from the car? And if it was? What should she do?

'Hey,' he said. 'Is it *this* road?' His finger running along the map.

Tracy swallowed her fear and looked. 'N – no,' she said. 'You've got the map round the wrong way. Woodfree Abbey is in the other direction.'

The man laughed. 'I'm so dumb,' he said. 'But these English roads don't help. Everyone driving on the wrong side. But I guess you're used to that, huh?'

'Pretty much,' said Tracy.

'Say, I couldn't twist your arm to help me with my car, could I?' He pointed. 'It's only a couple of streets away, back there.'

'I don't know anything about cars,' said Tracy.

'It wouldn't take a minute,' said the man. 'I just need someone to stand round the back and check my brake lights are working.'

'I'm sorry,' said Tracy. 'I've got to meet some friends.' She glanced at her watch. 'I'm late already. They'll be wondering where I've gotten to.'

'Oh, I'm sure they won't mind if you kept them waiting a few minutes longer,' said the man in a much lower voice. He snaked his arm round her shoulders and leaned close over her. 'You make one sound, young lady, and I'll break your neck.'

He tightened his grip on her and Tracy could feel the muscles of his arm taut round her shoulders.

'Now just keep smiling and you'll be OK.' His voice hissed in her ear. 'Try screaming and you're a dead girl. Got me?'

Tracy stared in horror into his face.

'I've got a gun,' he said, still smiling that terrible, cheery smile. 'And, believe me, I'll use it if I have to. Do we understand each other?'

'Yes,' murmured Tracy. 'But what do you want?'

He laughed. 'I want you to come and help me with my car.'

Holding her tightly against his side, and still smiling, he led her away from the main street.

Holly and Belinda stood outside Annie's Tea-room.

'We're a bit early,' said Belinda, peering in through the window. The small shop was filled with afternoon customers sitting at the little round tables with their white cloths, pouring tea and eating sandwiches and scones from shiny china plates.

'I can't see her anywhere,' said Belinda, her eyes resting longingly at the tempting confections on the sweet trolley. 'We could always go in and wait.'

Holly looked at her watch. 'Tell you what,' she said. 'We've got time to go to the department store and get you some make-up for tonight.'

Belinda stared round at her. 'I thought you were joking about that. I don't wear make-up.'

'Well, it's about time you did,' said Holly, sliding her hand under Belinda's arm and steering her away from the window. 'If you're going to get all dolled up so you can wear that necklace this evening, you'll have to wear make-up whether you like it or not.'

'I'd rather have a chocolate éclair,' said Belinda, casting her eyes back regretfully at Annie's Tea-room. 'And we don't want to miss Tracy, do we?'

'We have plenty of time,' said Holly. 'Stop squirming. I'm taking you to the department store

94

if I have to drag you every inch of the way.'

'I haven't got any money,' said Belinda.

'Yes, you have. Don't pretend. Look, do you want to look good tonight or not?'

'Do you want an honest answer?'

Holly laughed. 'No, not really. But, seriously, Belinda, you've got to look the part tonight. You've already agreed on a dress. A bit of make-up will make all the difference. Don't worry, I shan't get you up looking like a clown. Trust me.'

With profound reluctance, Belinda allowed herself to be pulled along the pavement and into the large, brightly lit department store.

An immaculate sales assistant glided up to them.

'May I help you?' she enquired.

Belinda gave her a dull look.

'Yes, please,' said Holly cheerfully. 'My friend here would like some make-up for a special occasion.'

'Certainly,' said the assistant, smiling. 'If you would just step this way.'

Belinda gave Holly a devastating look as she was led off.

'I hate you,' she whispered. 'I'm going to hate you for the rest of your life!'

Tracy was thinking quickly. The man said he had a gun. It would be crazy not to believe him. But right at that moment, with the map in one hand and his other arm round her shoulders, he couldn't easily get at it.

The question was: could she get away from him before he could get to it? And would he really shoot her?

She thought of Scheherazade's multimillion dollar turnover. A new design from Scheherazade could be worth a small fortune all on its own. Yes, she thought desperately, he *might* well think that sort of money was worth the risk.

But to allow him to take her to his car and drive her off who knows where? No. Not on your life, thought Tracy. Not without one heck of a fight.

He turned her into the pedestrian area. Just a little way ahead of them was Annie's Tea-room. Tracy almost groaned. Half an hour later and Holly and Belinda would have been there. They'd have seen that she was in trouble. But it was too early.

'There's a good girl,' he said. 'You just keep behaving yourself and everything's going to be fine.'

A mother with a push-chair came out of Annie's Tea-room in front of them, bringing them to a halt.

'He's dropped his teddy bear,' said Tracy, sliding suddenly down out from under the man's arm. She picked up the fallen toy and held it out to the infant's clutching hands.

The man stepped sideways to catch hold of her again, but Tracy spun round behind him and ran into the tea-room.

A large woman was on her way out. Tracy cannoned into her with a gasp.

'Do you mind!' boomed the woman. 'Really!'

Tracy felt a hand on her shoulder and something hard jabbed into the small of her back.

With a snort, the woman pushed past them.

It was too late. The man had her again. Her escape bid had failed.

'Out!' whispered the man in her ear.

A young waitress in a gingham dress came up to Tracy.

'Would you like a table?'

'Yes, please,' said Tracy. The hard object jerked into her back. She didn't need to be told that it was the man's gun.

'Follow me,' said the waitress.

'Very clever,' whispered the man savagely. He smiled over Tracy's shoulder. 'A table at the back, please,' he said aloud.

There was such a crush in the small shop, that no one noticed how close Tracy and the man were keeping as they made their way to a small empty table at the back of the tea-room.

He sat Tracy down in a corner, leaning over her so that she caught a glimpse of grey metal under his jacket.

'You're not going to show me up now, are you, Tracy?' he said for the benefit of the waitress, who was hovering with her notepad.

'No.'

'That's a good girl.' He sat down opposite her, the hand that held the gun pushed down under the tablecloth. With his other hand he picked up the menu card and passed it to Tracy.

'Have anything you like, honey,' he said. 'This is my treat.'

Tracy didn't want anything. Her stomach was in knots. But her only hope was somehow to keep him there until Belinda and Holly turned up.

They'd see her. They'd get help.

She ordered tea and a scone and the waitress wafted away.

The man leaned towards her, smiling his deadly smile.

'Now, listen here,' he whispered. 'You drink your tea, you eat your cake, we pay the bill, and we leave. You try anything else and you'll regret it.'

'You don't frighten me,' murmured Tracy, relieved that the fear that was tying her stomach in knots wasn't noticeable in her voice.

'If you ever want to see Judy again, you'll behave yourself,' said the man. He laughed softly, seeing the shock on Tracy's face. 'That's right,' he said. 'I guess you've got the picture now.'

'I won't do anything,' said Tracy.

Perhaps she wouldn't have to. If only Holly and Belinda would arrive.

They sat in deadly silence until the waitress returned with their order. Tracy glanced towards the door. Where were they? Where were Holly and Belinda?

She picked up the teapot and began to pour. She stiffened, catching a glimpse of Belinda's face through the window. Tea poured jerkily into her saucer.

'Watch what you're doing,' said the man.

She blinked at him.

They were there! They were outside the shop!

Tracy risked another glance at the window.

People at the table between her and the window stood up, preparing to leave, obstructing her view of the window, making it impossible for Belinda to see her.

Tracy caught a momentary glimpse of Holly over someone's shoulder. But that was all.

Her heart sank.

As the door to the tea-room opened to let the customers out, she saw clearly that Holly was pulling Belinda away from the shop.

They hadn't seen her.

They were going away from the shop without the least idea that she was inside and in danger.

'I think we've been here long enough,' said the man.

Tracy nodded dumbly. Perhaps if they left quickly enough her two friends might still see her.

Although it was only a minute or two, it seemed to Tracy to take forever for the man to pay the bill.

'Remember what I said,' he whispered as they

99

came out into the bright sunlight. 'No more tricks.'

Tracy looked around, feeling the man's grip once again on her shoulder.

It was an agonising moment for Tracy as she saw her two friends again. They were going into the department store.

All they had to do was look round.

Holly! Belinda! cried Tracy inside her head. *Look round!*

But it was too late. Her two friends went into the department store and Tracy realised that her last hope of rescue had gone with them.

She allowed herself to be led away from the pedestrian area and down into a narrow side street.

It gave her a cold feeling in her stomach as she saw the green car again.

'Get in.' The man opened the passenger door. She sat in the car. 'Seat belt,' he said. 'We don't want you having any accidents.'

As quick as lightning he circled the car and sat in the driver's seat.

'Where are you taking me?' asked Tracy.

'Don't try my patience,' said the man, inserting the key into the ignition.

She looked hard at him. 'Who are you?'

He smiled round at her, taking his sunglasses off. He had bright blue eyes.

'Who am I?' he said. 'And here's me thinking what a smart kid you were.' His mouth spread in a wide, mirthless grin. 'Don't you know?' He revved the engine and steered the car out into the road. 'I'm your uncle's right-hand man. I'm one of the brightest lights in the entire Scheherazade organisation.' He gave a chilling laugh. 'I'm Tony Meyer. And you, Tracy, you're about to help me make my fortune.'

8   Where's Tracy?

Holly wandered around the ground floor of the department store, waiting for Belinda. The attractive shop assistant had towed Holly's reluctant friend around various counters, explaining to her about eyeliner and mascara and blusher and lipstick. It was a good thing she didn't spot the silly faces Belinda was pulling behind her back. Holly had had to keep her lips pressed tightly together to stop herself bursting out laughing.

In the end, Holly had drifted off to have a look round at some of the other areas.

You never know, she thought to herself, eyeing the milling customers, *I might spot a shoplifter*.

She didn't.

She looked at her watch. Time was getting on. By now Tracy would almost certainly have finished her business at the police station, and was in all probability waiting for them in Annie's Tearoom.

Holly was leaning over a glass-topped counter displaying watches with brightly-coloured faces, when a hand landed on her shoulder.

102

'Got you,' said a husky voice. 'I saw you stuffing that deep-fat chip-fryer in your pocket. You'd better come quietly, miss.'

Holly looked round. Belinda was carrying a plastic bag with the department store's logo on it.

'You're making a terrible mistake,' said Holly. 'I'm a personal friend of the chief of police. Ask anyone.'

'They all say that, miss,' growled Belinda. She brandished the bag under Holly's nose. 'I hope you're satisfied,' she said in her normal voice. 'I've got enough stuff here to paint a barn.' She showed Holly the back of her hand, striped with browns and tans and deep pinks where the assistant had experimented on her.

'We'd better be getting off,' said Holly. 'Tracy will wonder where we've got to.'

They headed for the exit.

'It's not my fault we're late,' said Belinda. 'That woman wouldn't stop.' She shook her head. 'She's raving mad, you know. I told her I wanted something to go with a chestnut horse, and she just looked at me as if I were demented.'

'I'm not surprised,' said Holly. 'I don't suppose they get many people like you in here.'

They came out into the sunlit street and made their way towards the pedestrian area.

'Ask me how much this little lot cost me,' said Belinda.

'OK,' said Holly. 'How much did it cost?'

Belinda gave her an agonised look. 'Don't ask,' she said.

Holly laughed. 'You wait till this evening,' she said. 'It'll be worth it. You'll see.'

Annie's Tea-room was packed. They stood just inside the door, rising on tiptoe to scour the place for Tracy.

'I can't see her,' said Holly. 'She should have been here about twenty minutes ago.'

'Perhaps she got fed up waiting,' said Belinda. 'You know what she's like.'

'No,' said Holly, peering around from table to crowded table. 'She said she'd wait.'

A waitress approached them.

'I'm afraid we're full at the moment,' she said. 'Would you like to wait?'

'We're supposed to be meeting someone,' said Holly. 'A girl about our age, with blonde hair and blue eyes. I don't suppose you've seen her?'

The waitress looked meaningfully round at the throng and shook her head. 'We've been busy all day,' she said. 'I really couldn't tell you.'

'Oh. OK, then,' said Holly. 'Thanks anyway.'

A couple of middle-aged women rose from a nearby table, obviously preparing to leave.

'We'll sit there,' said Belinda.

Holly looked at her. 'Tracy's probably already gone home,' she said. 'There's no point in us hanging around.'

'Isn't there?' Belinda said determinedly, heading for the vacated table. 'There's some chocolate gâteau that says differently. I need fortifying after my ordeal.'

Holly laughed.

It was a good half hour before Belinda felt sufficiently recovered for them to leave Annie's Tea-room and head back to the Hayes' house.

It was like entering a three-ring circus. With Belinda's mother as the ringmaster.

The party caterers had arrived and were setting up tables in the long back room where the party was to be held. Wherever Holly and Belinda stood they seemed to be in the way.

They stuck their heads round the door of the party room. Trestle tables with white cloths ran down one wall with ranks of bottles and glasses at the ready.

'Those are my mother's secret weapons,' said Belinda. She grinned at Holly. 'That's what she does, you know, my mother. Gets them all tipsy and then hits them for big fat cheques.'

'Don't be silly, dear,' said Mrs Hayes, manoeuvring her daughter out of the way. Despite her harassed expression, Mrs Hayes still managed to look immaculate. Holly had never seen Belinda's mother with even a hair out of place.

'Is there anything useful we can be doing?' asked Belinda, hoping for a negative reply.

'Just keep out of everyone's way, dear, at the moment,' said Mrs Hayes. 'There'll be plenty to do a little later on.' She glanced into the party room. 'No, no!' she cried, bustling off to do some organising. 'I said I wanted all the chairs around the walls.'

'I don't think we're needed,' said Belinda. 'Fancy some ice-cream?'

But the kitchen was as chaotic as the front of the house. They couldn't even get to the freezer for piles of foil-wrapped plates and bowls.

They spent a few minutes down at the end of the Hayes' long garden, visiting Meltdown and giving him a quick groom.

'You must be forever keeping him clean,' said Holly.

Belinda grinned. 'It's a labour of love.' She patted Meltdown's sturdy neck. 'Isn't it, boy? Except when you take me through quagmires and come home plastered in mud like yesterday.' She looked at Holly. 'Remember?' she said. 'I came back with all that white goo all over me from that empty house?' She laughed. 'And that was nothing to the state *he* was in.'

'Should we give Tracy a ring, do you think?' asked Holly. 'I'd like to know what went on at the police station.'

'Good idea,' said Belinda.

They trudged up to the house.

The chaos had not abated. In fact it seemed to

have got worse. Mrs Hayes was talking on the phone and someone was in the party room tuning the grand piano.

Belinda and Holly hovered. Mrs Hayes was sitting in a quiet corner with the telephone in her lap.

They waited until she put the receiver down.

'Can I make a call?' asked Belinda.

Mrs Hayes shook her head. 'Not now, dear,' she said. 'I've got endless people to phone.'

Holly and Belinda looked at each other.

'Is it OK if we nip over to Tracy's house for half an hour?' asked Belinda.

Mrs Hayes looked at her, aghast. 'No, it isn't,' she said. 'There's too much to do here. I'm trying to contact your father. If I don't keep reminding him about the party, he's bound to turn up late, or forget to come home at all. You know what he's like. It's not often he's home for these dos as it is. Really, Belinda. There are any number of things you and Holly can be helping me with.'

Before Belinda could say another word, Mrs Hayes had given her a list of tasks as long as Meltdown's hind leg.

'We can always phone Tracy later,' said Holly. 'I'm sure she'll get in touch if anything interesting has happened.'

'If she can get through on the phone,' said Belinda gloomily. 'And as if it weren't bad enough having to do *this* all afternoon, I've still got to get myself dolled up for this evening.' She looked at Holly. 'It's a terrible life.'

'Come on,' said Holly. 'You'll enjoy it.'

Belinda gave her an expressive look, as though *enjoying* it were the last thing she was expecting.

Holly stood back as Belinda peered at herself in the mirror.

'It's no good,' said Belinda. 'I can't see a thing.' She crammed her spectacles on her nose and looked again. 'That's not *me*!' she exclaimed.

In the early part of the evening the two girls had taken themselves off upstairs to prepare for the party.

Expecting a busy day, Holly had brought her party things over that morning, when they had come to the Hayes' house to lock the necklace away. So it was only a case of carefully unfolding her dress from her bag and letting it hang for a few minutes to get the creases out.

It happened every time Holly looked into Belinda's bursting wardrobe. She was always amazed.

'Why do you never *wear* any of these things?' she said enviously. 'I'd love to have even half of the stuff you've got.'

'Take your pick,' said Belinda. 'In fact, take the lot. You'd be doing me a favour.'

'I don't think any of them would fit me,' said Holly.

'Are you suggesting I'm too big?' said Belinda in an affronted voice.

'No,' said Holly with a smile. 'I'm too small.'

'Do I have to wear this lipstick?' said Belinda.

'Yes.'

'It tastes peculiar.'

'You're not supposed to eat it,' said Holly. 'You've got it all over your front teeth. Here, let me do it.'

Belinda pushed her mouth out and Holly carefully applied the lipstick.

'Oony oot oocy oosn't ooned,' said Belinda.

Holly stared at her. 'What?'

Belinda relaxed her mouth. 'I said, it's funny that Tracy hasn't phoned. I thought we'd have heard something by now. I'll try phoning her, I think.' She dug her extension phone out from under a pile of things and lifted the receiver.

'Oh, sorry, Mum,' she said, putting it down again. She looked at Holly. 'She's *still* nattering away. No wonder we haven't heard from Tracy. She's probably been trying to call us all afternoon.'

'There can't be anything urgent to report,' said Holly. 'She could just cycle over here if there was. But I'm a bit puzzled that the police haven't been over to have a look at that necklace. You'd think they'd want to see it, wouldn't you?'

'I'm glad they haven't,' said Belinda, adjusting the bodice of her dress. 'That would have completely ruined our plans.'

'One small thing has been bothering me,' said Holly. 'What's your mother going to say when you swan in dripping with expensive-looking jewellery? I mean, she's bound to notice.'

'No problem,' said Belinda. 'I'll just tell her I borrowed it from the theatrical props at school. Don't worry about it. It's not as if it's real, is it?'

'No,' agreed Holly. 'Although for all the trouble it's caused, it might as well be.' She looked thoughtfully at her friend. 'I still think it's a lot of trouble for someone to be going to for one fake necklace,' she said.

'You know what Tracy said. A new Scheherazade collection can be worth a lot of money if you can steal the designs and sell them yourself.'

'Yes, I know,' said Holly. 'But this isn't a *collection*, is it? It's just one necklace. If someone wanted to pretend *they'd* designed them all, they'd need more than one necklace, wouldn't they? They'd need the whole lot.'

'We don't know that they haven't got the whole lot,' said Belinda. 'This might have been the only one Judy had time to send off before she was caught. I wish you'd stop inventing new problems all the time.'

'Sorry,' said Holly. 'I shan't say another word. Are you ready now?'

'I don't know,' said Belinda. 'Am I?'

Holly looked appraisingly at her.

Despite the fact that Belinda felt as if she were

110

dressed up like a particularly gaudy Christmas tree, she actually looked very good in her long red dress, and with her face carefully made up by Holly, and her hair brushed and shining.

'You'll do,' said Holly.

They heard the echo of the doorbell.

'That's the first of them,' said Belinda. 'We'll give it half an hour, and then we'll nip down to my dad's study and get the necklace out of the safe.' She grinned broadly. 'You know,' she said. 'I'm almost looking forward to this after all.'

'Good heavens!' Mr Hayes stood open-mouthed in the hall, a champagne glass in his hand and an astonished expression on his face.

'Hello, Dad,' Belinda said with a grin.

As she and Holly had emerged from the study, Belinda had seen her father chatting to some new arrivals in the hall.

'Belinda!' gasped Mr Hayes. 'What have you done to yourself?'

'Like it?'

He shook his head in amazement. 'It's like a butterfly coming out of its cocoon.' He beamed at Holly. 'Did you have a hand in this?' he said. 'I can't imagine Belinda did it all on her own.'

'I helped a bit,' admitted Holly.

'Well, I'm speechless. You look . . . both of you look . . .' He shook his head again. 'Very presentable indeed. Has your mother seen you?'

111

'Not yet,' said Belinda. 'And don't get carried away, Dad. This is a definite one-off. It's back to sweat-shirts and jeans in the morning.'

Mr Hayes looked more closely. 'Is that one of your mother's necklaces?' he said. 'I can't say I recognise it.'

'I borrowed it,' said Belinda. 'It's only paste.'

'Well, it looks very fine on you, Belinda.' He nodded approvingly and turned back to the people he had been speaking to.

'That's it,' whispered Belinda. 'Interview over. Let's go and mingle.'

The confused sound of voices, all seeming to be speaking at once, flowed out of the open double doors of the party room. It had been transformed since the two friends had last seen it. The room was teeming with people in their best clothes, every one of them apparently trying to be heard above the cacophony.

Over in one corner a young woman was playing the piano, background music that could only just be heard above the noise.

'So?' whispered Holly. 'Who are the jewellers, then?'

'I've no idea,' said Belinda, staring into the mêlée. 'They're not going to have labels on, are they?'

'I thought you might know some of them.'

'Well, yes, I might,' said Belinda. 'Let's wander around a bit and see if I recognise anyone.'

Belinda's idea of wandering around involved making a beeline for the tables laden with food at the far end of the room.

'Hello, Belinda,' said a woman in a vivid green gown. 'You're looking unusually attractive tonight. I don't think I've ever seen you in a dress before.'

Belinda smiled politely and moved on, Holly following in her wake.

'If anyone else says that, I'm going to go upstairs and change into my jeans,' Belinda hissed at Holly. 'I'm sure everyone's secretly laughing at me.'

'Don't be so wet,' said Holly. 'Everyone thinks you're gorgeous.'

'Possibly,' Belinda said heavily. 'But I don't feel gorgeous. I feel distinctly silly.' She filled a paper plate with odds and ends and they moved away from the tables.

They edged themselves round the crowded room, trying to listen in on conversations.

'This is no good,' Holly said after a while. 'No one's noticing the necklace at all. You'll have to talk to people.'

'What about?'

'I don't know. What do you know about? You must know how to make small talk.'

'*You* make small talk,' said Belinda. 'All I know about is horses, and all this lot are rabbiting on about is money, so far as I can tell.' She craned her neck. 'Oh! Hold on. I think I recognise *him*.'

113

She nodded towards a tall, gaunt man with swept-back grey hair, chatting with a couple of people on the other side of the room.

'A jeweller?' whispered Holly.

'Yes. I think so. His name's Mudlark, or something.'

'Mudlark?' Holly said in astonishment. 'Are you sure?'

'It's something like that. He owns that big shop in Market Street. You know the one.'

'Medlock's?' said Holly with a laugh.

Belinda nodded. 'Yes, Medlock's, that's the one.' She looked at Holly. 'Well?' She said. 'Shall I go and flaunt the necklace at him?'

They were halfway across the room when they bumped into Belinda's mother.

'Hello, girls,' she said. 'Well, you look . . .' She gazed at Belinda. 'You look . . .'

'I think gorgeous is the word you're groping for,' said Belinda with a tight smile.

'I was going to say, a trifle overdressed,' said Mrs Hayes, staring at the necklace.

'Don't you like it?' asked Belinda.

'Oh, it's very nice,' said Mrs Hayes. She leaned conspiratorially close to Belinda. 'But people don't really wear things like that at informal occasions,' she said. 'It looks . . . out of place.'

'It's only costume jewellery,' said Belinda.

Mrs Hayes' eyebrows shot up. 'I know *that*, dear. That's the whole point. Oh, never mind, I haven't got time to give you a talk on etiquette.'

One of the men Mrs Hayes had been talking to leaned to look at the necklace.

'It's a very fine piece,' he said. 'I've been looking for something like that for my wife.'

Holly's ears pricked up.

'If you don't mind my asking, where did you get it?' he said with a smile.

'I borrowed it from the props box at school,' said Belinda.

The man frowned.

Holly felt a tingle of excitement run up her spine.

'I'm amazed,' said the man. 'You must tell me which school you go to. I'd like to have a look through their props box if it's full of things like that.'

Belinda laughed politely – she was getting used to laughing politely – and wandered away.

Holly caught up with her. 'That might be our man,' she whispered in Belinda's ear. 'Why didn't you talk to him some more?'

Belinda gave her a pitying look. 'Because he's the Assistant Police Commissioner,' she said.

'Oh.' Holly felt deflated.

'I'm peckish again,' said Belinda.

They made their way back to the buffet tables.

Belinda was about to pitch a forkful of coleslaw on to her plate when Holly grabbed her arm.

'Careful,' began Belinda.

'Listen,' hissed Holly. 'I just heard someone mention Scheherazade.'

115

Belinda looked cautiously round. Further along the table the man she had pointed out as being the owner of Medlock's, the jeweller's, was talking to another man.

'Are you sure?' whispered Belinda.

Holly nodded.

The two girls sidled along the tables.

'He'll end up in prison,' Medlock was saying. 'No doubt about it.'

The other man nodded in agreement. 'You'd think they'd be red hot on security, with things like that,' he said. 'I can't believe anyone would be so negligent.'

'Oh, that's the Americans all over,' Medlock said airily. 'If I'd borrowed items as valuable as that I'd hire an entire army to look after them.'

'Not that *our* royal family go about lending people jewellery,' said the other man.

Medlock laughed. 'Not to the likes of us, anyway.' He turned to pick up something from the table and his elbow nudged against Belinda.

'Oh, excuse me,' he said, glancing at her. His hand came to a halt in mid-air. For a split second his eyes locked on to the necklace, then he smiled and looked away.

Holly and Belinda looked at each other.

Had a flicker of recognition passed over his face in that instant he spotted the necklace? To be honest, Holly had to admit it hadn't. But she was certain that the snatch of conversation they had overheard was

116

something to do with the Scheherazade organisation. She was *certain* Medlock had mentioned the name Scheherazade a few seconds previously.

'We need to talk,' Holly whispered in Belinda's ear.

Belinda nodded and the two friends made their way across the party room and out into the hall.

'He *was* talking about Scheherazade,' Holly said urgently. 'But what do you think they meant about prison and negligence and all that?'

Belinda looked around. 'Not here,' she said. 'Let's go up to my room.'

Once in her bedroom, Belinda slammed the door and stood breathlessly with her back to it, her eyes wide.

'Don't you realise what they were saying?' she gasped. 'They were talking about royal jewels going missing. That's what Medlock meant when he talked about hiring an army of security guards. Royal jewels, Holly!'

'And Tracy told us that her uncle had borrowed some of the Thai royal jewels to make a collection of copies,' said Holly. 'The new collection. The originals must have gone missing. That's the only thing he can have meant.'

Belinda stared down at the sparkling necklace hanging at her throat. 'Oh, no,' she said. 'No. No, no, no. It *can't* be.' She looked in horror at Holly. 'It can't be, can it? Seriously, Holly, tell me it can't be.'

With trembling hands she unclasped the necklace from behind her neck and spread it on her upturned palms.

The diamonds winked up at her. The rubies burned on her hands. The delicate silver shimmered in the light.

'Of – of *course* not,' stammered Holly. 'Of course this isn't the *real* one. You'd be able to tell, wouldn't you? If they were real jewels, they'd be . . .' her voice trailed off.

'I know how to test for diamonds,' said Belinda, her voice shaking. 'Paste doesn't cut glass. Real diamonds do.'

They looked around for some glass.

'This will do,' said Belinda. It was a photograph of Meltdown, hanging on the wall above her bed. A photo behind a frameless sheet of glass.

Belinda jumped on to her bed and took the photograph down, scrabbling frantically to get the clips off.

Holly knelt next to her and the two girls held their breath as Belinda bunched the necklace in her hand and drew it slowly along the sheet of glass.

There was a soft, hissing, grazing sound.

The diamonds had left clear white strokes the length of the glass.

In the terrible silence the two girls slowly turned their heads to look at each other.

'Oh, *boy*!' murmured Belinda. 'Catch me, Holly. I think I'm going to faint.'

9 Another kidnapping

'Where are you taking me?' asked Tracy.

Tony Meyer's eyes, behind the dark of his sunglasses, didn't leave the road.

'California,' he said. 'You'll love it there. Sun, sea and sand.'

'Funny man,' murmured Tracy.

Tony Meyer grinned wolfishly. 'Ask a silly question,' he said, 'and you'll get a silly answer. Do you know that saying?'

'Yes,' said Tracy. 'And I know another one: Crime doesn't pay.'

Tony Meyer gave a yell of laughter. 'Don't you believe it, sweetheart. Don't you believe it. You're talking to a rich man, here, Miss Tracy Foster.'

'My uncle trusted you.'

'Your uncle's a fool,' Tony Meyer said with a grin. 'And while we're trading old sayings, have you heard the one about pulling the wool over people's eyes?' He glanced at her. 'I've been pulling the wool over your uncle's eyes for a long time. But this is the *big* one. This is where Tony Meyer takes the money and runs.'

They had been driving now for half an hour or so, Tracy guessed. The town of Willow Dale was far behind them and they were up in the rolling Yorkshire hills. The wide expanse of countryside was dotted with only the occasional house or farm.

She had tried her best to memorise their route, but the roads wound and switchbacked so often as they made their way through the hills, that she was afraid she was lost. And to make matters worse, she was becoming convinced that Tony Meyer was deliberately driving them round in circles, as if to make absolutely certain that she had no hope of guessing where they were headed.

In a long, lonely stretch of road, Tony Meyer suddenly pulled the car to the side and switched off the engine.

Tall bushes lined the road.

The sudden silence, after the continuous burr of the engine, was alarming.

'Any idea where we are?' asked Tony Meyer.

'No,' Tracy said quickly. She had a map in her head, and she hoped – *hoped* – that she'd remembered all the twists and turns right.

'You know, I'm not too certain I believe you,' Tony Meyer said with a grin.

'What are you going to do with me?' asked Tracy.

Tony Meyer leaned towards her, his face very close to hers, his eyes unreadable behind his sunglasses.

'Where is it?' he asked.

'I don't know what you're talking about,' mumbled Tracy.

Tony Meyer drew the gun out of his pocket and displayed it on his hand.

'See this?' he said.

'Yes.'

'OK' His face came even closer. 'Where *is* it?'

'I don't know what you're talking about,' said Tracy, desperately trying to keep her voice level. 'I haven't got anything of yours.'

'Oh, I think you have, Tracy,' said Tony Meyer. 'A little gift from your cousin Judy? *Now* do you know what I'm talking about?'

'The chocolates?' said Tracy.

Play dumb, Tracy, she thought to herself. *Convince him you don't know anything.*

Tony Meyer slid the gun back into his pocket.

'The chocolates,' said Tony Meyer. 'Tell me what you've done with the chocolate box and I'll let you out right here.'

'I don't know where it is,' Tracy blurted. 'I gave them away. I don't like dark chocolates.'

'I can't figure out whether you're stupid or just very brave,' said Tony Meyer.

'I'm not brave,' mumbled Tracy.

'No?' He thumped his hands loudly on the steering wheel. 'Get into the back!' his voice rasped suddenly.

'Sorry?'

'Get into the back. Climb over the seat. Come on, move yourself. I've had enough of your nonsense.'

Tracy undid her seat belt and pulled herself over the back of her seat. Tony Meyer leaned over her, pulling up a length of rope from somewhere behind his seat. He quickly tied Tracy's wrists and ankles, jerking at the ropes to pull her on to her back on the long seat. He yanked a blanket out from under her. The last thing Tracy saw before he draped it over her head, was that wicked, cold, mocking smile.

The blanket was stifling. It smelt musty, as if it had been in an attic for years. As the car moved along, bumping over the uneven roads and swerving around bends and corners, Tracy was flung about helplessly on the back seat.

The discomfort of her position was so acute that she hardly had time to think about anything else. At first she had tried wringing her wrists together, hoping to loosen the knots. In films when the hero was tied up, the knots always came loose at some useful point. But Tracy wasn't in a film; she was bundled up in the back of a car travelling who knew where with a dangerous armed man at the wheel.

She tried to occupy her mind by remembering the turns that the car made. When it turned right, her head bumped against the door. When it turned left, it was her feet that hit against the side.

Count the bumps, she thought. Three bumps to the left. One to the right. She rolled forward slightly. They were going down a hill. Another head bump. A roll back against the back of the seat. Uphill. Bump to the left. Shuddering and jarring. That must mean a particularly rough stretch of road. A length of uneven roadway going downhill.

But would she be able to make sense of all this information once she'd got herself out of this?

The length of time they had been driving would suggest that they were miles and miles from Willow Dale. Unless, as she had guessed earlier, Tony Meyer was still going round in circles to disorientate her.

The car slowed and she heard a new sound. A quite new noise echoing up through the bottom of the car. Not the hard grind of wheels on tarmac. Something louder and somehow softer, she thought. Gravel. The crunch of gravel, punctuated by wet-sounding noises. As if they were driving through puddles.

The noise of the engine suddenly stopped. Tracy lay quite still, listening intently. Now what?

She heard the driver's door open and, a few seconds later, felt cool air seeping through the blanket as the rear door was pulled open.

She felt Tony Meyer lean across her. She gave a gasp of relief as she felt the ropes being loosened from her ankles.

'Out!' Tony Meyer's voice commanded.

'I can't,' gasped Tracy. 'I can't move.'

She was lifted by the shoulders and the next thing she knew she was standing on crunching soft gravel. Or not quite gravel. More like gritty mud. Wet, oozy, gritty mud.

The blanket was arranged over her head so that she still couldn't see where she was. Through the thick, coarse material she could tell that it was still light. So they hadn't been driving *that* long.

She was pushed from behind. She heard the car door slam.

The mud sucked at her shoes as she stumbled blindly forward.

'There's a step here,' said Tony Meyer.

Her foot hit against the step and she almost fell. A strong hand gripped her arm.

'Careful,' said the chilling voice. 'You don't want to hurt yourself.'

She heard the creak of a door and as she was pushed forward the light dimmed and the atmosphere changed.

She was in some sort of building. That much was obvious. But what building? And where?

Her footsteps, and those of her captor, echoed strangely. As if they were in a big hall. And the smell. A dank, sweet smell that made her think of old cellars. The sickly smell of dry rot.

Tony Meyer led her deep into the building. He pushed her backwards. The backs of her knees struck against something hard and she collapsed on to some sort of seat.

At last he pulled the stifling blanket away.

Tracy blinked at him.

They were in a dilapidated room. Wallpaper was hanging off the walls in damp strips. Daylight filtered bleakly through filthy window-panes. There were a few items of damaged, dirty furniture and a table that had been drawn into the centre of the room.

Tracy glanced upwards. Half the ceiling seemed to have caved in and she could see rotten joists through the remaining scraps of plaster. And above the joists she could even see into an upper room through missing floorboards.

This was no ordinary house. The ceiling was high. It had to be a derelict mansion house of some sort. There were a few of these lonely old mansions scattered about the hills. Relics of a bygone age, when people could afford to live in this sort of luxury. Not that there was anything luxurious about her surroundings now. If this room was anything to go by, the whole building was just about to come tumbling down around her ears.

Tony Meyer had his back to her, at the table. For a moment she wondered what he was doing. But then she saw him lift a portable telephone and punch out a number.

He held the phone to his ear.

In the silence she could faintly hear the purr of the phone.

There was a long pause.

'Damn!' said Tony Meyer, slamming the phone down.

He looked round at her, his eyes piercing her now that he had taken his sunglasses off. Piercing, wicked blue eyes beneath frowning brows.

Tracy gazed levelly at him, waiting for him to speak.

'Damn!' he muttered again.

He walked agitatedly to the window and stared out.

'What have you done with Judy?' asked Tracy, her mouth terribly dry.

'Shut up,' he said. He strode back to the table, snatched up the phone and dialled again.

Tracy watched him. Up until then he had seemed horribly cool and calm. Obviously the lack of an answer from whomever he was trying to call was rattling him.

He let the phone ring for a long time before bringing it crashing down on to the table again.

'My mom will have missed me by now,' Tracy said softly.

He spun round and once again she felt the chill of his pale blue eyes on her.

'Then you'd better put her mind at rest, hadn't you?' he said. He picked up the phone again. 'What's your number?'

126

Tracy recited the number to him. He moved close to her, listening at the receiver. 'Tell her you're OK,' he said. 'Tell her you're out with your friends.'

He crouched at her side, turning the phone so Tracy could speak into it, but so that he was still able to hear what was said at the other end.

'Hello?' It was her mother's voice.

'Mom?' said Tracy. 'It's me.'

'Tracy! For heaven's sake, girl, where have you been?'

'I'm OK, Mom,' said Tracy, shivering at the way Tony Meyer's eyes were fixed on her. 'I – I went for a bike ride with Holly. We got a bit carried away. We've been miles. It'll be a while before I can get back, Mom. I didn't want you to worry.'

'Where are you? Are you all right?'

'Yes, yes, I'm fine. Holly got a flat tyre, that's all. I'll be home soon, Mom.'

'Tracy! I can't believe you've *done* this. We were . . .' Tony Meyer pulled the phone away from Tracy's ear and put his hand over the mouthpiece.

'Say goodbye,' he whispered.

He put the phone back to her mouth.

'I've got to go, Mom. I'm in a phone booth and there's someone else waiting to make a call.'

'But, Tracy—'

'Bye.' Tony Meyer's hand came down on the button to cut the line.

He stood up. 'OK,' he said, staring down at her.

His eyes were so sharp. As if he could drill through her head with them and read her thoughts.

He slid his hand into his jacket pocket. The pocket with the gun in it.

'And now,' he said with icy calm. 'We've got to decide what we're going to do with you.'

10   A desperate ride

'You're not really going to faint, are you?' asked Holly.

'I *should* do,' said Belinda. 'I've just spent the evening strolling around with a couple of hundred thousand pounds worth of stolen royal jewels around my neck.' She stared at Holly. 'For heaven's sake,' she said. 'I even showed them to the Assistant Police Commissioner.' She began to giggle, holding her hands over her mouth.

'It's not *funny*,' said Holly.

'You don't have to tell me that,' said Belinda, her face becoming solemn again.

'No wonder these people were so desperate to get their hands on it,' said Holly. She jumped off Belinda's bed and picked up the telephone.

'There's no need to call the police,' said Belinda. 'The Assistant Chief Thingamajig is only downstairs.'

'I'm not calling the police,' said Holly. 'I'm calling Tracy. We can't just hand this necklace over without her even knowing what's been going on. She'd murder us.'

Belinda waited as Holly held the phone to her ear.

'Oh, it's their answering machine,' said Holly, quickly putting the phone down. 'They must be out.'

'Out? Out where?' said Belinda. 'I thought she said they'd both be sitting at home by the phone in case of any news about Judy.'

'I know,' said Holly. 'But their answering machine was on all the same.'

'You don't think anything could have happened to them, do you?' said Belinda. 'I mean, like the burglars coming back?'

This was a nasty thought. Holly's quick imagination conjured up a picture of Tracy and Mrs Foster lying bound and helpless on their living room floor.

'We'd better go down and tell the Commissioner about this, Holly,' said Belinda.

Holly nodded.

They had just come to the top of the stairs when Belinda suddenly grabbed Holly's arm and pulled her back.

'Look!' she whispered.

The two girls peered through the banister. At the far end of the hallway, by the front door, the tall, grey-haired figure of Mr Medlock was standing talking to Mrs Hayes.

'Must you go so soon?' Mrs Hayes was saying.

'I'm very sorry,' said Mr Medlock. 'Urgent business. It can't wait, I'm afraid.'

'What's he up to?' whispered Belinda. 'Why is he off so suddenly?'

'Do you think he recognised the necklace?' said Holly.

Belinda nodded fiercely. 'I'll bet you anything you like he did,' she said. 'Quick, come with me.'

The two girls ran helter-skelter along the upper hall. The Hayes' house was a huge, rambling affair, and Holly had only ever seen a few rooms of it. Belinda was leading her to the back of the house.

'What are we up to?' panted Holly.

'Out the back way,' said Belinda. 'To see what he does.'

They rounded a corner and ran down a narrow flight of stairs. Belinda hauled at a bolt on a door and the two friends came running out into the cool darkness of the evening.

They circled the house. The driveway was full of cars. They saw Mr Medlock walking briskly towards them, a deep frown on his face.

'Back!' whispered Belinda. They were only just in time. As their heads ducked out of sight Mr Medlock opened the door of a car only a few feet from where they were standing.

Belinda edged an eye round the wall. Medlock was sitting in the car, its door slightly open. He was punching numbers into a car phone.

Belinda could clearly hear the staccato rap of his

fingers on the dashboard as he waited for his call to be answered.

At last. 'It's Medlock,' he said into the phone. 'Don't talk. Listen. I've seen it. Yes. Yes. It's here. Listen to me, you fool. What?' There was a brief pause. 'What do you mean, you've been trying to contact me all afternoon?' Another short silence. 'What? You've done *what*? Kidnapped her? Are you quite mad, Meyer? The girl hasn't got it any more, we already knew that. It's *here*, at that stupid Hayes woman's house. I don't know. I don't know how it got here.'

Another pause. 'No, you fool. Of course I can't get it. The place is crowded. Yes. Yes. It's definitely the right one. Do you think I'm as big an idiot as you are? It's the one in the photograph you showed me. Definitely. Listen, Meyer, will you *listen* to me for one second? All right, all right, calm down, man. I'll be right over. Yes, I'm calling you from the car. I'll be fifteen minutes at most. But you listen to me, Meyer, you got me into this, and you'd better have a damn good idea how to get us out again.'

Belinda saw him throw the phone down and pull the car door closed. As the car manoeuvred out of its parking space something very interesting met her eyes. The mudguards and wheels of Medlock's car were spattered and smeared with white mud.

The car vanished through the gateway and the

two girls came out into the open.

'He called my mother stupid,' Belinda said. 'She won't like that much.'

'He called the other person *Meyer*,' said Holly. 'He was talking to Tony Meyer. So Medlock must be the other man from the car that tried to grab Tracy. And the American *was* Tony Meyer, just like Tracy thought. But what do you think he meant about the *girl*? He said they knew the girl didn't have it.'

'Judy, of course,' said Belinda. She gave Holly a grim smile. 'And I think I know where they've got her,' she said.

'What?' Holly stared at her in amazement. 'How could you possibly have worked that out? He didn't mention any place names.'

'He didn't have to,' said Belinda. 'I figured it out all by my observant self.' Belinda grinned. 'Remember the white mud I came home covered in yesterday after I'd been out with Meltdown? His car was splashed with the same stuff.'

'You said it was from the driveway of a big house. But there could be any number of houses with that stuff in the drive.'

'Oh, no, there aren't,' Belinda said without any trace of doubt in her voice. 'You forget, newcomer, I've lived all my life around here. I know all the places within easy riding distance. And that was the only place I've ever seen with that nasty gunk in the drive.'

133

Holly clapped her hand to her head. 'And that green car,' she said. 'The hired car from outside Tracy's house last night after the burglary. Don't you remember? I said that had white wheels. I wrote it down. White wheels. But it wasn't white wheels at all. It was that same mud.'

'We're on to them, Holly,' Belinda crowed. 'Right, it won't take us ten minutes to get over to Tracy's place.'

'You don't think we should tell the police first?'

'In your dreams!' said Belinda. 'We'll tell *Tracy* first. The three of us, remember? The Mystery Club. All for one and one for all, and all that stuff. Come on, let's get changed. You can use my spare bike.'

Holly hesitated.

'Come *on*,' said Belinda. 'The longer you stand there dithering, the longer it'll be before we've got this mystery solved!'

'OK, I'm coming.'

They ran up the back stairs and quickly tore off their party clothes.

'Think how great Tracy is going to feel when she can tell everyone she was right all along about Judy,' said Belinda, hopping on one leg as she fought her way into her jeans.

'And think how relieved Judy will be when she gets rescued,' added Holly, pulling her jumper on. 'Right. I'm ready. Let's go.'

'Hang on,' said Belinda. 'I'll try Tracy's place

134

once more on the phone.'

'If the answering machine's on, just leave a message,' said Holly. 'You never know, people sometimes leave the answering machine on when they're at home, just to save having to talk to people if they're in the middle of a good programme on television.'

Belinda dialled.

'Tell her we know where Judy is,' said Holly. 'What's the name of the place?'

'I don't remember,' said Belinda. 'Something beginning with H, I think.' She looked at Holly. 'It's ringing,' she said. 'H? Hollymere? No, that's not right. Halfmoon House?' She shook her head. 'Handmere? Hardmoor? Haremire? Haremire sounds right. Oops – yes, it's the answering machine again. I hate these machines. They ought to be made illeg—' She cleared her throat and spoke rapidly into the phone. 'Ah! Um. Yes. Hello, the Fosters' answering machine, this is Belinda calling for Tracy. We've had a breakthrough. No time to tell you all about it now. We're coming over, in case you're there. You'd better be there, Tracy. Or you'd better get back there pretty quickly. You'll miss everything otherwise. We're dead certain that Judy is being held at . . .' She hesitated, still not certain that she had remembered the name right. 'Haremire House,' she said, looking at Holly and shrugging.

She dropped the receiver into its cradle.

'And if Tracy's not there, we go straight to the police,' said Holly.

'You're on,' said Belinda. 'Now! Let's go!'

The Fosters' house was in complete darkness. Mrs Foster's car was parked outside, but there was no sign of life through the darkened windows.

Belinda and Holly had come racing up on their bikes, skidding to a halt and rushing up to the front door, pressing the doorbell so that it rang wildly through the house.

'I don't like this,' said Belinda, trying to see through the glass panels in the door. 'There's no sign of anyone at all. But the car's there. Where can they have got to?'

'I've had a really horrible thought,' said Holly. 'Remember when Medlock mentioned the *girl*?'

'Yes. Judy. So?'

'No,' said Holly. '*Not* Judy. Remember – he was shocked about something Meyer had done. He wouldn't be shocked to hear that Judy had been kidnapped. He must have known about that already. I've got the most horrible feeling that he was talking about Tracy. They've got Tracy.'

'I hope you're wrong,' said Belinda. She chewed her lip. 'If we go across the fields we can be at that old house quicker than if we go back to my place to raise the alarm.'

'Can you find your way like that?' asked Holly. 'Over the fields *and* in the dark?'

'Can fish swim?' said Belinda.

'Yes, they can,' said Holly. 'But that doesn't mean – Belinda! Where are you going?'

'No time to lose,' said Belinda, running down the path.

'But what can we do if she *is* there?' called Holly, as Belinda ran out on to the pavement and wrestled her bike up from the ground.

'Rescue her!' yelled Belinda.

'Belinda! Wait!' But there was no stopping her friend now.

Holly leaped astride her bike and followed Belinda as she rode at breakneck speed into the night.

The full moon hung milk-white in the starry sky. In any other circumstances Holly would have loved just to lie down in the long grass to gaze up at the twinkling lights. But on this particular night, neither Holly nor Belinda had any time to spare for stargazing.

It had been the most hectic, frantic, bone-shaking bike ride of Holly's life, following in Belinda's wake over the tumbled fields and hills. She would have yelled out for Belinda to stop and give up if she'd had enough breath. As it was, it took all her concentration just to stay upright, as the bike threatened to skid away from under her and send her nose-diving into the mud.

Grimly determined, Holly trailed the bobbing

red light of Belinda's bike up steep, agonising slopes and down terrifying falls of hummocky grass into unguessable pools of darkness.

But Belinda seemed to know exactly where she was going.

They came to a crest of moonlit grassland and, at last, Belinda came to a halt.

They hung over the handlebars, gulping in the cool night air, their heads reeling from the exertion.

'There . . .' gasped Belinda. 'That was . . . a piece . . . of . . . cake . . .'

'Never again . . .' panted Holly. 'Never, ever again.'

Belinda straightened up in the saddle, her feet stretched to support herself, and sucked in a few deep, steadying breaths.

'Stop complaining,' she said. 'We're nearly there now. Look.'

In the darkened valley below them, Holly could make out the hunched shape of a large house. A grey streak of road led to the front and, quite clearly in the moonlight, Holly saw the eerie white shine of the driveway.

And even at that distance, they could make out the black shapes of two parked cars, like pools of black water in the pale mud.

'Let's go for it,' said Belinda, nudging the front wheel of her bike over the rim of the hill.

Holly nodded and they started the final, bone-jarring ride down into the valley.

11 The deserted house

'Come with me.' Tony Meyer strode towards the door of the derelict room. To Tracy's relief, he had taken his hand out of the pocket of his jacket. The pocket in which she knew he had put his gun. He turned at the door and glared at her.

'Do I have to carry you?'

Tracy shook her head. She stood up and followed him, her legs still aching from the ropes that had bound her in the back of his car. She sensed that this wasn't a good time to say anything. The failure to get any answer from whomever he had been attempting to contact by phone had clearly unsettled Meyer.

His accomplice, thought Tracy. *The other man in the car. The Englishman.*

Now that she was no longer blinded by the blanket, Tracy could see that her guess about the house had been right.

He pushed her along a corridor and they came out from behind a wide main staircase into what was obviously the front hallway of the mansion. Through the dirt and rubble that littered the floor

Tracy could see broken patterned tiles.

Tony Meyer's fingers poked into her back. 'Up the stairs,' he said.

The boards creaked as she went up the stairs. Specks of dust hung in the air in the slanting light of the late afternoon.

One thought kept circling in Tracy's mind: if he had intended doing her any harm, he could have done it by now. He wanted information out of her. That's why he had brought her here. He wanted to know where the necklace was.

He pushed her up another flight of stairs. She caught glimpses of empty rooms and corridors leading off.

A third flight, more narrow than the others. She guessed they were coming to the top of the house. It was the sort of staircase that led to an attic, and at its head was a small lobby leading to a single closed door, bolted at top and bottom.

Roughly taking hold of her by her tied wrists, he stooped and wrestled the rusty lower bolt open.

'I don't know where the necklace is,' said Tracy, shuddering at the thought of being locked away up here.

It was a mistake. She realised that instantly. Up until she had spoken, there had been a chance that Tony Meyer might have believed she thought the box from Judy had contained nothing other than chocolates. Now he knew better.

'So?' he said. 'You found the necklace?'

'You'll never get it now,' said Tracy. 'It's been handed over to the police. They know all about you.'

'Do they?' he said, his fingers biting savagely into her wrist. 'Is that a fact? *All* about me, huh? Well that's pretty clever of them, Tracy. How do these British policemen work? By telepathy? Because *you* didn't know anything until I picked you up.'

He loosened the second bolt and jerked the door open.

'Let's see if you can't come up with a better story. There's a guy coming here soon. And believe me, Tracy, I'm a pussycat compared to him. He'll get the truth out of you.'

He gave her a savage push and she stumbled forward into darkness, the door slamming behind her. She heard the sound of the bolts being shot home and the creak of his feet on the stairs as he descended.

Well done, Tracy, she thought. *You and your big mouth.*

She strained her eyes into the gloom, waiting for them to adjust to the thick darkness. Gradually the room began to resolve itself in the faint grey light from a low window that seemed to have a sheet of sacking or something tied across it.

There was no furniture, save for a filthy mattress spread on the floor in one corner. The walls rose to about four feet then angled inwards, shaped by the slope of the roof. A closed door led off to the left.

Floorboards groaned as she walked across to the door.

If I'm going to be stuck up here, I might as well have a look around, she thought as she turned the handle. *At least I can try to find something to cut these ropes.*

She turned the doorknob and pulled the door open towards her. She heard a stealthy sound from beyond the door. There was a rush of noise, and something large came sweeping out of the darkness, grazing across the top of her head as she instinctively ducked.

'Eat that, you creep!' It was a girl's voice. With an American accent. A fierce, angry voice that shouted out of the darkness of the hidden room.

'Judy!' yelled Tracy. She glanced up. Something long and solid was swinging to and fro above her head in the doorway.

'Who's there?'

'Tracy!'

'Tracy?' A pale face appeared around the edge of the doorway. 'Ha-haah!' The voice whooped.

The reunited cousins hugged each other.

'Rescued!' Judy shouted, squeezing Tracy breathless in her embrace. 'I thought it was that creep Meyer.' She looked up. A floorboard, suspended from ropes, swayed inches above their heads. 'You're lucky you're not taller,' said Judy.

'You'd have gotten my booby trap right in the teeth.' She grabbed Tracy's hand. 'Let's get out of here.' And then she noticed the bonds that held Tracy's hands together.

'This isn't a rescue,' Tracy said miserably.

'What?' The joy fell from Judy's face. 'You mean . . .? Oh, great! They got you as well? That's really great. Well done, Tracy.' Judy looked eagerly into her cousin's face. 'Did you get the necklace?'

'I got it.'

'Did you take it to the police?'

Tracy bit her lip. 'N – no . . . not exactly . . .'

'Tracy!'

'It was a while before we even realised there was anything in that box,' said Tracy. 'You should have sent a note.'

'I did,' shouted Judy. 'I put a note with it telling you to keep them to yourself. Heck, Tracy, you've got to be the dumbest thing on *earth*! And I mentioned Harry over the phone. Didn't you realise something was *wrong*?'

'Of course I did,' said Tracy, becoming angry in her turn. 'But everyone was telling me you were OK. How was I supposed to know what was going on?'

'I should have called Mickey Mouse!' shouted Judy. 'At least he might have gotten me out of this, instead of getting himself *caught*!'

'Don't yell at me, Judy,' cried Tracy. 'I've been burgled and grabbed at out of cars and dragged

143

here at gunpoint. I didn't come here out of choice! I thought that guy was going to shoot me.' She lifted her hands. 'The least you can do is untie me.'

Judy's voice calmed. 'OK,' she said. 'OK, I'm sorry. I guess you wouldn't have known what Meyer was up to.' She worked rapidly at the knots and in a few seconds Tracy was free to massage her numbed wrists.

Tracy smiled grimly. 'I've figured it out now,' she said. 'It's your dad's new collection, isn't it? Meyer was going to sell Scheherazade's new collection to a rival company.'

Judy stared at her. 'You don't know, then?'

Tracy looked puzzled. 'I don't know what?'

'The necklace, Tracy. It isn't a *fake*. It isn't one of my dad's copies. It's the *real thing*.'

Tracy leaned heavily against the doorway, her head spinning. 'I think you'd better run the whole story by me, Judy. What *exactly* is going on here?'

The cousins were sitting on the mattress. Judy had pulled down the sacking from over the window, and they could see the sky beginning to darken towards evening.

'My dad's known that someone was ripping the company off for months,' explained Judy. 'There's been an internal investigation, and everything. He thought maybe it was one of the designers. You know, some greedy guy creeping off and selling the new ideas to rivals. The only person he trusted completely was Tony Meyer. It was Meyer who ran the investigation. *That's* how much Dad trusted him. And it was Meyer who came up with the idea of borrowing the Thai royal jewels. It sounded like a great idea. My dad was real excited. Meyer arranged everything. The transfer of the jewels to the company, the security for looking after them once they were there, *everything*. Which was how he was able to do the switch.'

'But how did you find out?' asked Tracy.

'It was on the aeroplane,' Judy continued. 'I knew Meyer was supposed to have a selection of copies in his case. That was why he was coming over to England in the first place. To show the designs at our London office. A kind of sneak preview. No one had seen the designs. No one except my dad, Meyer and the guys who had actually made the things. It was that secret. Even I hadn't seen them.'

'You're kidding!' said Tracy. 'Your dad wouldn't even show them to *you*?'

Judy smiled ruefully. 'I haven't been getting along too well with my folks recently,' she said. 'Heck, you know what it's like.' She looked anxiously at Tracy. 'I'm sorry,' she said, remembering that Tracy's parents were divorced. 'I guess you *don't* know.'

'I can imagine,' said Tracy. 'Go on.'

'Well, we'd been having arguments, you know? That's why I didn't want to go on that camping vacation with them. That's why I asked if I could come over and stay with you. I had this big fight with my dad a couple of weeks ago. We haven't spoken to each other since. I guess he wouldn't let me see the new designs as a kind of punishment.' Judy shrugged. 'He can be like that.'

'So what happened?'

'Well, I knew Meyer had the copies – what I *thought* were the copies, in his briefcase. I knew he wouldn't have risked putting them with his other luggage in the cargo hold. So I waited until he had to use the rest room, and I opened the case to have a look.'

'Oh, I see,' Tracy couldn't hide the tone of disapproval in her voice.

'Don't get all holier than thou on me, Tracy,' said Judy. 'I know I shouldn't have, but I kind of couldn't help myself. I was so mad at my dad. And I only wanted a quick look.'

'And you realised they were the real jewels?'

Judy grinned. 'Not all of them. Everything except the necklace was a Scheherazade copy. You see, they always stamp the letter S somewhere on their designs. It's a kind of trademark. Well, they all had this S on them except the necklace. I thought it was odd. And then' – her voice lowered – 'I tried scratching the face of my watch with it. And it *cut* it, Tracy. It cut the glass face of my watch. I saw Meyer coming back, so I put all the other stuff back in the bag and put the necklace in

146

my pocket. I guessed right away what was going on. I thought that if I could stall him until the plane landed, I'd be able to get to the police.'

'But why didn't he steal the whole lot? Why only the necklace?'

'I guess he thought that would be too obvious. He needed time to get away. He must have hoped that no one would notice that the jewels he'd handed back to the Thai royal family had one fake among them. At least, not right away. And on its own that one necklace is worth hundreds of thousands of dollars. Enough to set him up for life if he got away with it.'

'And he saw you, did he?'

'He didn't say anything, but I could tell he was suspicious of me. He must have seen I'd moved his case. I bought the chocolates from the duty free cart and went off to the rest room. That's when I put the necklace in there. So that if he *had* seen me and he searched me, he wouldn't find it. Well, we got to the airport and suddenly he wasn't this nice guy I'd known all my life any more. It was real creepy, Tracy, the way he changed. He let me go to a post office and send you the box, but he was with me all the time. I couldn't get away from him to alert the police or anything. And then he got real nasty. He took me to a hotel. He was so mad when he found out I didn't have the necklace any more. He said he'd keep me there until I told him what I'd done with it.' Judy looked unhappily at her cousin. 'So I had to tell him. He could have done anything, Tracy.'

'So what did he do then?'

'He made a couple of phone calls. One to New York. To some accomplice of his. Telling them that if they got any phone calls about me they were to say I was OK.'

'The emergency phone number,' said Tracy. 'I called it, and the guy said exactly that – that you were OK and I shouldn't worry.'

'And then he phoned someone else. Someone in England. He locked me in the bathroom, so I didn't hear anything. He obviously had it all planned. That was when he got me to make my phone call to you. He showed me the gun and said if I didn't do exactly what he told me, I'd know what to expect. And the next thing I knew we were on a train up here and I was locked in this place.' Judy gave a rueful smile. 'My last hope was that you'd figure out something was wrong and get the necklace to the police.'

Tracy looked hopefully at her cousin. 'It could still be all right,' she said. 'My friends Holly and Belinda have got the necklace. Once they realise something's happened to me, they're bound to tell the police.' Tracy put an arm comfortingly around her cousin. 'Don't worry, Holly and Belinda will save us.'

'Yes,' Judy said darkly. 'Just like you saved me.' She smiled. 'But I don't intend sitting around up here to be saved, Tracy. I want out of here.'

'The door's bolted,' said Tracy. 'And we're too high up to climb out of a window.'

She stood up and looked out over the lonely dales. 'We can't even signal to anyone. There aren't any houses for miles.'

'Come with me,' said Judy. 'I've got an idea.'

Tracy followed her into the other room. Judy pointed upwards. There was a square trap-door in the low ceiling.

'I guess it must lead somewhere,' said Judy. 'I couldn't reach it on my own, but if you give me a leg up I should be able to manage it.'

Tracy looked up at the trap-door and grinned. 'It sure beats sitting around waiting,' she said.

She linked her hands together and braced herself as Judy took hold of her shoulders and pushed herself upwards.

Tracy staggered under the weight as Judy's hands shoved at the trap.

'Got it!' cried Judy. Tracy heaved upwards with her hands and Judy managed to get a hold through the opening trap. A second later and Judy's legs were scything in the air as she pulled herself up.

Judy stretched herself out flat in the roof space and reached down for Tracy's arms.

It was pitch black up there, but the floor seemed solid enough as they crawled cautiously away from the dim light of the trap-door.

Tracy coughed in the dust, feeling blindly for

149

her cousin. Cobwebs, or something equally unpleasant, brushed her face, hanging from the invisible slope of the roof just above their heads.

'Judy?'

'I'm here. Follow me.'

'I can't see you.'

'Grab a hold of my foot. I think I can see some light up ahead.'

Slowly Tracy and Judy edged their way through the darkness. They came to a low stretch of brickwork and climbed carefully over it.

'We must be above another room by now,' said Tracy.

'Sure we are,' said Judy. 'Ha! Look at that!'

Tracy raised her head. There was a square of pale light in the floor a few metres ahead of them.

They peered down into an unfamiliar room. The trap-door in the ceiling of this room had obviously fallen in. They could see it lying on the floorboards.

One after the other, they jumped down into the deserted room.

'Way to go!' crowed Judy. She ran to the door. 'I'm out of here!'

'Don't make so much noise,' hissed Tracy. 'Don't forget Meyer's got a gun. We don't know where he might be.'

Judy looked round at her and nodded. 'I haven't forgotten,' she said. 'I'd like to get even with that guy.' She opened the door. It led to another narrow flight of stairs that stretched down into half-darkness.

They crept down the stairs, wincing every time a board creaked under their feet.

'How long, do you think, before Meyer comes up to check on us and finds we're missing?' asked Tracy.

'I don't know,' said Judy. 'He's been bringing me food first thing in the morning, and then again in the evening.'

They padded across a hallway and looked out through a wide window. It overlooked the front of the house. They could see Meyer's green car in the drive, and a snake of roadway winding through trees towards a glimpse of a distant tarmac road.

'He's expecting someone,' said Tracy. 'He was trying to get hold of them on the phone.' She gazed out at the darkening sky. 'He probably won't go up there until the other guy arrives. Do you know who he is?'

'I've never seen him,' said Judy. 'He's English, though, I know that much. I heard them talking.' She grinned at Tracy. 'And he's scared.'

'Scared?'

'Yes. They were talking on the stairs outside the room they had me locked in,' said Judy. 'The English guy was trying to convince Meyer to drop the whole thing and run. He was saying that he didn't like all this kidnapping business.'

'What did Meyer say to that?'

'He said: "While I've got the gun, you'll do what I tell you." That kind of settled the argument.'

'I don't like the idea of having to cross all that open ground,' said Tracy. 'We don't know where Meyer is. We're going to be in real trouble if he spots us.'

'What else can we do?' asked Judy. 'I don't trust our chances of overpowering him. He's no weakling.'

'I think we should wait until it gets a bit darker,' said Tracy. 'We've got a better chance of getting away without being seen once it's dark.'

'OK,' said Judy. 'Let's find ourselves somewhere to hide.' She grinned. 'That's a good idea of yours, Tracy. Even if he goes up to check on us and finds we've escaped, he's not going to think we're still in the house.'

They slid silently along the corridor, looking for a room to hide in and wait for darkness to fall.

It was no fun sitting silently in a dirty corner of an empty room. Hardly daring to speak in case Tony Meyer was prowling the house within earshot. Hardly daring to stretch their cramped legs for fear of sending tell-tale creaks from the rotten floorboards echoing out into the slowly gathering gloom.

Judy seemed to have coped with her imprisonment remarkably well, but Tracy was concerned for her.

She tried to take Judy's mind off their predicament by whispering stories to her about how the Mystery Club always came through in the end. She couldn't help it, she thought, if she made it sound as if she was always the one who saved the day. She wasn't doing it on purpose – it just came out that way.

They stared at each other as a sound broke the silence. The noise of an approaching car. They heard it stop and clearly heard the bang of a closing car door.

'It's the other guy,' hissed Tracy. 'It must be.' She looked at her watch. It was so dark now that she had to hold it close to her face.

'Shall we go for it?' said Judy.

Tracy nodded.

It was terrifying, after all that caution, to set out into the impenetrable gloom of the night-dark house.

'We'll go out the back way,' said Tracy.

They were right out at the back of the house, looking for a way down to ground level, when they suddenly heard a distant beeping noise.

'What's that?' asked Judy, her eyes wide. 'The police?'

'No,' said Tracy, shaking her head. 'It doesn't sound like a police siren. I think it sounds like a car alarm.'

'Are you sure?' asked Judy.

Tracy nodded. 'We could go and check, I suppose,' she said.

They made their way towards the front of the house. A loud bang stopped them in their tracks. It sounded like a gunshot.

'What was *that*?' hissed Judy.

'Do you think Meyer's shooting at someone?' said Tracy.

There was only one way to find out. As they crept across the floor of one of the rooms at the front of the house, the beeping noise suddenly stopped.

They looked at each other.

'Weird,' said Judy.

They crept to the window. There were two cars now in the drive, but they could see no sign to explain what the noises they had heard could mean.

'Let's get out of here,' said Tracy. 'Before someone comes up here and catches us.'

In the upper hallway, Tracy suddenly stopped, motioning at Judy to do the same.

They could hear a distant hissing.

'It's the hurricane lamp,' whispered Judy. 'Meyer uses it at night. There's no electricity in this place.'

'That's good,' said Tracy. 'We'll know where he is.'

They continued their stealthy way along the hall. Light flickered dimly through an open doorway.

They tiptoed towards it. The light was coming

up through missing floorboards, sending strange shadows up on to the ceiling.

Holding her breath, Tracy edged towards the gaping rent in the floor.

The hurricane lamp was set on a table and, standing with his gun in his outstretched hand, was the foreshortened figure of Tony Meyer.

Tracy came down silently on all fours, twisting her head to see down into the lower room.

She had to bite back a gasp of shock.

From this vantage point she could clearly see who it was that Tony Meyer was menacing with his gun.

It was Holly and Belinda.

12 Caught!

Holly and Belinda walked their bikes round to the back of the house. Lofty dark walls towered above them, punctuated by dead-eyed windows.

'Haremire House, indeed!' whispered Holly.

Belinda looked round at her. 'I can't be expected to get everything right,' she said.

They had ridden down the long hill into a line of tall trees. Peering out from the darkness under the branches, they had seen a board lying by the side of the drive.

In large gothic print they had read the words 'Hawkmoor House'. So even if anyone did get to the Fosters' house and listen to the answering machine message, they wouldn't be able to help. They'd be looking for a place called Haremire House. A place that didn't even exist.

Belinda rested her bike against the wall. 'I knew it was named after an animal of some sort,' she whispered at Holly. 'I got that much right.'

'An elephant is an animal of some sort,' hissed Holly. 'And anyway, a hawk is a bird, not an animal.'

Belinda frowned at her. 'Birds are animals.'

Holly gave her a ferocious look. 'Are we going to stand here arguing about it?'

Belinda shrugged and crept towards the back of the house, muttering to herself about how unreasonable people could be, and how she was always expected to do *everything*.

They sidled along the wall, their hearts beginning to hammer in their chests.

Holly still had no real idea of what they had expected to accomplish by coming here. Belinda seemed to have it in her head that they would be able simply to pile in and snatch Judy from under the very noses of her captors. Holly wasn't at all sure about this. All she wanted to do was get a clear look at the man from the green car, to make certain their suspicions were correct, and then to get to a phone as quickly as possible and call for some help.

Twigs crackled under their feet. The dead remnants of some plant that had once grown alongside the wall.

'Shhhh!' hissed Belinda.

'I'm being as quiet as I can,' mouthed Holly.

They came to the corner of the huge house. Moonlit grass that had once been a lawn stretched away into the distance. A strange shape lifted itself out of the grass. A statue, or a dried-up fountain, probably, thought Holly. Beyond the grass they could see only the sinister dark of trees or tall bushes.

Belinda halted suddenly and Holly bumped into her.

'Listen,' said Belinda.

Holly strained her ears. Apart from the thudding of her own heart, she could hear nothing.

'What's that noise?' whispered Belinda. 'Can't you hear it?'

'No. What noise?'

'A kind of hissing noise,' said Belinda. She leaned to tip her head round the edge of the brickwork. 'Ahhh!' she said.

Holly stretched her head round Belinda's shoulder. A small square of shaggy grass was illuminated by a patch of light thrown down from a window several metres along the back wall.

'I know what it is,' said Belinda. 'It's a hurricane lamp. We use them in the stables.'

'Of course,' said Holly. 'This place can't have electricity, can it? They'd need something so they could see at night.'

They moved along the wall, passing a sunken doorway, and edging themselves towards the window from which the light spilled.

Crouched below the window, their eyes met as they heard the sound of voices.

'That's our pal Mudlark,' Belinda breathed, recognising Medlock's voice. The other voice spoke in an American accent.

158

Broken panes of glass made it possible for the two girls to hear clearly what was passing between the two men.

They were having an argument.

'I want nothing more to do with this, Meyer,' said Medlock. 'You should have given it up the moment that girl found out about the necklace. All I had to do was find someone willing to sell the stuff. That's what you told me. I wasn't prepared for anything like *this*! When the girl got away from us last night, we should have given up. This is just madness.'

Holly nudged Belinda. So it *was* Meyer behind everything.

'I'm getting tired of your whining,' said Meyer. 'So you just want to cut and run, do you? Leave me to pick up the pieces, huh? Is that your plan? You were glad enough about your share of the money when we started all this. I didn't hear any whining from you then.'

'That was different. Look, I don't care what you do. Just leave me out of it. I've got no stomach for this sort of thing. Threatening young girls.' Medlock's voice took on a desperate edge. 'You'll never get your hands on that necklace now. Give it *up*, Meyer, for pity's sake. Before the police track us down.'

Meyer laughed harshly. 'Before they track *you* down, I think you mean,' he snarled. 'You seem to forget. The girl knows who I am. I can't just go back home as if nothing's happened. I'm in this all the way. And if I'm in it all the way, then so are you, Medlock. So instead of standing there shaking in your shoes, I suggest you help me think of a way out of this mess.' His voice took on a more menacing tone. 'And come up with some idea about what we're going to do with those two girls.'

Holly nudged Belinda's arm and gestured for her to follow her. Out of earshot of the window, she whispered in her friend's ear, 'Let's find a telephone.'

Belinda nodded. They knew enough now. Meyer had spoken of two girls. Judy was one, and they were convinced that the other must be Tracy. Both of them were locked up somewhere in the house, with Meyer desperate enough to do anything to save himself.

So long as the two men kept arguing, the captives were safe. But Holly didn't think the argument sounded like it was going to last much longer. It sounded very much as if Meyer was getting sick and tired of Medlock. And once Medlock had been dealt with, what would Meyer's next move be?

There was no time to lose.

They ran soft-footed round to where they had left their bikes.

'Where's the nearest house?' asked Holly.

'A couple of miles away,' said Belinda.

They wheeled their bikes round to the front of the house, secure in the knowledge that Medlock and Meyer were safely out of sight in that back room.

'Just a minute,' said Holly. 'Medlock had a phone in his car. If we could get at that, it would be much quicker than cycling a couple of miles.'

Their bikes left trails in the oozing white mud as they made their way over to Medlock's car.

Holly peered through the side window.

'Can you see it?' asked Belinda.

'Yes! Look!' It was lying between the front seats. Holly tried the car door handle. It was locked.

'Break the window,' suggested Belinda.

'What with?'

'I don't know. Your *head*,' complained Belinda. 'There must be a rock or something lying about.'

They looked around. The grainy white mud lay all about them. Belinda propped her bike against the side of Medlock's car and ran off to the grass verges, stooping and feeling through the undergrowth.

They had turned their bike lamps off as they had come down the hill, to ensure that their approach was not seen by unfriendly eyes in the house. Holly glanced down at her darkened lamp. She had an idea. She eased the front lamp out of its cradle between the handlebars. It was plastic, but it was quite hard.

She laid her bike down, stepped back and threw

the lamp with all her strength at the car's side window.

There was a loud bang as the lamp bounced ineffectually off and splashed into the mud.

Belinda's anxious white face stared out of the gloom.

'Holly!' came a loud hiss. 'Why don't you fire off a few rockets while you're at it?'

'I was trying to break the glass,' Holly said in a loud whisper. 'I can't break glass quietly.'

'I've found something,' said Belinda.

Holly glanced apprehensively round at the front of the house. The doorway was shrouded in darkness. Would they have heard the noise?

Belinda came running over, clutching something. She showed it to Holly. Half a brick.

'Quick!' cried Holly.

Belinda planted her feet firmly in the mud, swung her arm back and flung the brick with a breathless gasp.

It missed the side window, striking the windscreen and ricocheting off the bonnet.

A piercing electronic scream shook the still night air. Holly hardly had time to register the spiderweb of cracks that Belinda's ill-aimed missile had made on the windscreen, as the two girls scrambled for their bikes.

The two men may not have heard the noise that the brick had made, but no one could be deaf to the frantic screeching of the car alarm.

The two girls tumbled over each other in their rush to escape. Dragging her bike up, Holly collided with Belinda. One arm of her handlebars meshed into the spokes of Belinda's front wheel and both bikes came crashing into the mud, Holly losing her balance and pulling Belinda down with her.

They scrabbled to get to their feet.

'Are you OK?' gasped Holly.

'Yes, yes,' panted Belinda.

They fought to get the bikes apart, but the brake wire from Holly's bike had got itself tangled in Belinda's spokes.

'Leave them,' Belinda shouted. 'Run!'

They heard a crash from behind them and a blaze of white light flared out on to the drive.

Holly glanced over her shoulder. Medlock was in the doorway, bathed in the fierce light of the hurricane lamp that he held aloft in one hand.

But more dangerous than that was the silhouetted figure of Meyer, leaping down the broad front step and running towards them.

The two girls took to their heels.

'Stop!' shouted Meyer. 'I've got a gun. Stop!'

The terrible crack of the gun being discharged split the night, louder even than the clamour of the car alarm.

The girls came to a skidding halt and turned to face Meyer. His arm was raised. He had fired into the air. A warning shot.

He walked towards them. 'Get inside,' he commanded. 'Now!' He waved the gun at them.

He walked behind them into the house.

'Turn that damned thing off,' he spat at Medlock. The car alarm was still wailing at full volume.

But Medlock was staring at Holly and Belinda as if he couldn't believe his eyes.

'It's them!' he said. He pointed at Belinda. 'She was the one wearing the necklace!'

Meyer sat on the edge of the table, his cold blue eyes on the two girls in front of him. He held the gun loosely in his hand, not threatening them directly with it, but making it clear that he was in command of the situation.

Medlock stood nervously by the door, his eyes flitting from the girls to Meyer.

'You'll never get hold of the necklace now,' Holly said defiantly.

'Is that so?' said Meyer. 'I'd have thought your folks would be prepared to trade the necklace to get you back in one piece.' He reached behind himself and lifted the portable phone from the table. 'One phone call ought to do it.' He looked at Medlock. 'You know this area,' he said. 'We need to choose a pick-up point. Somewhere we can get away from once they've handed the necklace over.'

Medlock stared at him with bulging eyes.

Meyer's face deepened into a deadly frown. 'Medlock?'

164

'Yes – yes,' stammered Medlock. 'I'm trying to think.'

'Think quick,' said Meyer. His eyes turned to the two girls. 'Who knows you're here? Anyone?'

'Yes,' Belinda blurted. 'The police. They're right behind us.'

Meyer laughed softly. 'I don't think so,' he said.

'The police . . .' murmured Medlock in obvious fear. 'The police?'

'You coward,' spat Meyer, staring at Medlock. 'The police aren't coming. This pair wouldn't be here if they'd called the police. Now think, you spineless piece of misery, where can we arrange to pick up the necklace?'

'There is a place,' mumbled Medlock, his thin grey face running with sweat. 'Barnard's Corner. It leads straight to the motorway. But—'

'Shut it!' said Meyer. 'You can fill me in on the details later.' He walked over to Belinda, the gun in one hand and the phone in the other. 'Call your folks,' he said. 'Tell them to drop the necklace off at Barnard's Corner.' He looked at his watch. 'In an hour. Tell them they'll never see you again, otherwise.'

Gathering all her courage, Belinda shook her head.

'No,' she said. 'I won't do it.'

Meyer lifted the gun. 'I think you will.'

'Meyer,' gasped Medlock. 'You can't!'

'I told you to shut it,' said Meyer. 'Do you think

I'm not prepared to kill these kids to get my hands on that necklace? Do you think I've been playing *games*, Medlock?'

'I won't let you harm them,' gasped Medlock, lurching forward, his arms stretched out as if he meant to try and take the gun from Meyer's hand.

Holly winced as Meyer's arm swung with snake-like speed and the edge of the gun struck the side of Medlock's face.

Medlock crumpled backwards to the floor, his hand to his cheek, an expression of shock and pain on his face.

'One more word,' snarled Meyer. 'One more *movement* from you and you *get* it.'

Medlock crawled away from him, his eyes glassy with fear.

'Call home,' said Meyer, thrusting the phone towards Belinda.

'It's no good,' said Belinda. 'Even if I *did*, it's no good. They don't know where the necklace is. I'm telling you the truth.'

'Then you can tell them where to look for it,' said Meyer.

'I can't,' gasped Belinda. 'It isn't at my house any more.'

Holly caught hold of Belinda's hand. 'Tell him. For heaven's sake just *tell* him,' she said. 'He won't hurt us if he gets the necklace.'

Meyer forced the phone into Belinda's hand.

'Do as your friend says,' he said. 'Just get me

that necklace and you're home free.' His heavy hand came down on Belinda's shoulder. A sudden change came over his face as his fingers moved towards Belinda's neck. A look of excitement and almost disbelief. He yanked at the neck of her sweat-shirt.

There, hidden until that moment by the neck of her sweat-shirt, lay the sparkling necklace.

'Belinda!' gasped Holly.

'I thought it would be safer than leaving it,' Belinda said dully. She undid the clasp and reluctantly let the shimmering necklace down into Meyer's outstretched hand.

A look of greedy triumph spread over Meyer's face and he began to laugh, clutching the necklace in his fist.

'I guess you won't have to call home after all,' he said.

'You've got the necklace,' said Holly. 'So you can let us go now.'

Meyer pushed the jewellery into his pocket, backing away towards the table.

'I'm not so sure about that.' He slowly raised his arm so that the gun was pointing directly at the two girls. 'I'm not so sure about that at all.'

13   A sudden attack

'Geronimo!' Tracy's whooping war-cry echoed down into the derelict room. Tony Meyer had just enough time to flick his eyes upwards before Tracy's full weight came crashing down on him.

Belinda and Holly let out simultaneous yells of surprise and delight as Tony Meyer collapsed under Tracy's sudden attack.

There had been no time for Tracy to think, wonder or worry about the outcome of her leap through the floor of the upper room. Holly and Belinda were in danger; that was all that mattered to her in the fleeting moments between seeing the peril that her friends were in, and launching herself, feet first, through the hole left by the missing floorboards.

And what an attack!

Tony Meyer went down like a house of cards, the gun spinning out of his hand as he was driven into the floor with a stifled yelp of shock.

Holly sprang forwards and snatched up the gun from where it had come to rest against the wall.

Whatever happened next, at least Meyer was weaponless.

But Tony Meyer was in no condition to retaliate, with or without his gun.

He lay crumpled motionless on the floor as Tracy sprawled breathless, arms and legs everywhere, on his back.

A voice cried down from the ceiling. 'Way to go, Tracy!'

Belinda looked upwards and saw a grinning girl's face staring down at them through the rent in the ceiling.

A second later the face vanished and Belinda heard the clatter of feet above them.

She ran to pull Tracy to her feet.

'Got him,' panted Tracy, leaning on Belinda's steadying arm. 'Phew!'

'Tie him up!' They looked round. Medlock was sitting up, his suit rumpled and patterned with dust. 'Quickly – tie him up,' repeated Medlock. 'The man is mad. Don't give him a chance to recover.'

Belinda knelt and twisted her head round to look into Meyer's face. Mouth open, eyes closed. Out for the count.

'I don't think he's up to much right now,' said Belinda.

Medlock heaved himself to his feet. 'He may be faking it,' he said.

'Faking?' said Belinda, looking incredulously

into Medlock's sweat-streaked face. 'He's unconscious.'

'Don't move!' commanded Holly, holding Meyer's gun stretched out towards Medlock in both hands. 'Don't do *anything*.' She hoped she sounded more convincing than she felt. There was no way in the entire world that she would have been able to use the gun, but she was relying on Medlock believing she *might*.

Medlock shook his head. 'Don't be stupid,' he said, pointing a shaking finger at Meyer. '*He's* the man behind all this.' He loosened his tie and pulled it out from under his collar. 'Bind his hands with this. Quickly, now.'

Tracy took the tie from him and knelt to haul Meyer's limp arms up across his back.

'I hope I haven't killed him,' Tracy said anxiously. 'I mean, he's OK, isn't he?'

'He's breathing at least,' said Belinda. She grinned at Tracy. 'That's what I call a *rescue*.'

Tracy tightened the knots and stood up.

Medlock seemed to relax slightly now that his former accomplice was tied up. 'You saved all our lives,' he said to Tracy. 'The man was getting madder by the minute. I think he might have shot us all.'

'Who *is* this guy?' said Tracy, staring at Medlock.

'His name's Mudlark,' said Belinda. 'You ought to recognise him. He's the one who tried to pull you into the car last night.'

170

'Medlock,' he muttered, frowning at Belinda. 'Not Mudlark.'

They heard feet in the hall and looked round as Judy came running in.

'You ought to be in *films*, Tracy,' she cried. 'I've never seen anything like it.' She grinned around at the girls. 'No wonder the Mystery Club made you their leader!'

'No wonder *what*?' exclaimed Belinda. She frowned at Tracy. 'What have you been telling her?'

'Shouldn't we call the police?' suggested Tracy, avoiding Belinda's challenging look.

'The police aren't on their way?' said Medlock.

'Not yet,' said Holly. 'But they will be in a minute.' She stooped to pick up the telephone from where Belinda had dropped it.

Medlock made a sudden leap forward, taking all the girls by complete surprise.

'Holly!' shouted Tracy. 'Look out!'

But it was too late. Medlock swept the gun out of Holly's hand before she even had time to register what was going on.

He turned and waved the gun. 'Get over by the wall,' he said, his face running with sweat. He glanced down at the telephone, brought his foot up, and stamped down hard on it. There was the crack of breaking plastic.

'Holly!' Tracy groaned. 'You *idiot*!'

Holly looked helplessly at the gun, trembling in

Medlock's hand. She hardly needed Tracy to tell her that her moment of being off her guard had put them all back in danger.

The girls backed away.

'You,' barked Medlock, looking at Belinda. 'Feel in his pocket. Take the necklace out. Quickly now.'

Belinda crouched by Meyer's side.

'Don't!' shouted Judy. 'Look at him. He's shaking like jelly. He'll never use that thing.'

'I will,' said Medlock. 'If you force me to.'

Belinda looked at Judy and then at the gun in Medlock's hand. She didn't feel like taking the risk. He looked nervous enough to fire the thing off by accident.

She drew out the necklace and stood up.

'Bring it over here,' said Medlock, reaching out his hand. 'Don't be scared. I shan't harm you. Just give me the necklace and I'll let you all go.'

'I've heard that one before,' said Belinda.

'The necklace!' commanded Medlock.

Belinda dropped it into Medlock's hand.

'Move away from me,' said Medlock. He began to sidle to the door.

Judy let out a sudden laugh. 'I don't *believe* this guy,' she said. 'He's threatening us with a gun, and he hasn't even taken the *safety catch* off!'

Medlock's eyes swivelled down to the gun. Judy made a sudden bound forwards, spinning and kicking high.

172

Medlock let out a yell of pain as her foot cracked against his hand and the gun went flying. He staggered back against the wall, clutching at his wrist.

Medlock's angry eyes bulged at them. Holly picked up the gun again, determined this time that no one was going to take it from her.

'Call the police,' she said.

Belinda looked down at the broken phone. 'How?' she said.

'Use the car phone,' said Holly.

'Yes! Of course!' Belinda ran to the door. 'Don't let him trick you again,' she warned.

'Don't worry,' said Holly. 'I won't!'

Belinda fumbled for a moment in the darkness of the hall, feeling for the handle of the front door.

'Ow!' She found it with the back of her hand. Hard. She shook her stinging hand, pulling the door open.

She ran towards Medlock's car, half-blind in the night after the glare of the light from the hurricane lamp.

The windscreen was webbed with cracks, but the glass was still holding. She searched for the brick. It had to be somewhere close by.

She found it and hammered it into the middle of the maze of cracks she had already made. There was a loud report as the windscreen shattered. Smashing out a hole in the windscreen, she leant over the bonnet and reached inside.

Stretching full length she grabbed up the car phone.

She stabbed out three nines and held the phone to her ear.

'Which service do you require?'

'Police!' yelled Belinda.

She nearly jumped out of her skin as the blare of a police siren filled the air. She spun round, her mouth open. With its motor roaring and its brakes screaming, a police car came hurtling into the drive. The doors were flung open and four police-men leaped out.

'That's what I *call* service,' gasped Belinda. She gabbled into the phone. 'It's OK – they're *here*!'

She threw the phone down. 'They're in there!' she cried, pointing towards the house. 'But . . . but how did you *know*?'

One of the policemen ran up to her. 'Are you all right? We had a call through about an abduction.'

'Yes, yes, it was me,' said Belinda. 'I mean, it *wasn't* me – it was Tracy – but – oh, never mind. They're all inside.' She ran along behind the policemen. 'One of them's unconscious and we've got the other one at gunpoint.'

They ran into the hall, the policemen's torches sending wheels of light skidding over the lofty walls.

'Where are they?' barked one of the policemen.

'This way,' said Belinda. 'Follow me.'

She pelted along the hall, the policemen following in her wake.

She came to a crashing halt in the doorway of the room where she had left the others, her mouth hanging open.

In the few minutes that she had been away, things in the room had changed completely.

When Belinda left to get to Meyer's car phone Tracy turned to gaze at her cousin in admiration. 'How did you *do* that?' she gasped, astonished at the athletic manner in which Judy had disarmed Medlock.

'Dance lessons,' said Judy. 'Pretty impressive, huh? High kicks were always my specialty.'

Medlock moaned and the three girls turned to look at him.

'You've broken my wrist,' he groaned, cradling one hand in the other.

'How?' said Judy. 'It was just a tap.'

'Don't go near him,' warned Holly. She looked down at the gun. 'How did you know the safety catch was on?'

'I didn't,' said Judy. 'But I figured he wouldn't either. I mean, look at him. Does he look as if he knows anything about guns?'

They looked at the gaunt man in his rumpled suit, his grey hair hanging over his eyes and his face streaked with sweat. He looked about as dangerous now as a rabbit caught in a car's headlights.

There was a groan from the floor. All eyes turned to Meyer. He writhed in the dust, heaving himself on to his side and blinking uncomprehendingly at them with glazed eyes.

'Stay where you are,' Holly said to him.

Judy walked over to him, her eyes bright with anger. 'I hope they put you away for two hundred years,' she said. 'I hope they lock you up and throw away the key.'

Holly caught a movement out of the corner of her eye. 'Medlock!' she shouted.

In the few moments that their eyes were off him, Medlock had edged to the door. Holly caught a glimpse of his black jacket as he vanished into the hall.

'He's still got the necklace!' shouted Tracy.

The three girls darted after him. He seemed to have forgotten about his wrist – broken or not – as he stumbled along the hall.

He glanced back at them for an instant, wheeled around the banister rail, and went crashing up the stairs, his face white with panic as he made this last desperate attempt to escape.

But pursuit was close at his heels. Tracy was only a couple of feet behind him and Judy was running in her wake.

Judy shot a glance back at Holly. 'Stay down there,' she shouted. 'In case he doubles back.'

176

Medlock came to the top of the stairs. He hesitated for a moment, as if realising that he'd be
trapped for sure if he didn't find a way down
again. He turned, looking as if he was ready to
charge the girls as they came up the stairs. Then he
seemed to change his mind as he saw Holly in the
gloom at the foot of the stairs with the gun in her
hand.

The girls stopped on the stairs, watching to see
what he would do next. With an angry shout, he
flung the necklace towards them and ran.

Tracy ducked.

'Got it!!' she heard Judy shout.

Tracy came up on to the passageway. Medlock
was running blindly. She saw him silhouetted in a
doorway for an instant. Then he ran forward.

There was a single yell of shock from him as she
saw him teeter for a second in the light that came
up through the missing floorboards. And then he
was gone.

Tracy heard a heavy thud.

'He's fallen!' she shouted. 'He's fallen through
the floor!'

The three girls ran back to the lower room.

Medlock was lying, groaning on the floor, one of
his legs twisted awkwardly under him.

Meyer had somehow got to his feet and was
standing, swaying dizzily over his fallen partner.
He backed away as the three girls ran into the
room, shaking his head, his eyes swimming.

177

Medlock looked pitifully up at the girls.

'It's my leg,' he gasped. 'I think I've broken my leg.'

Tracy crouched at his side. 'It's OK,' she said. 'Don't try to move. We'll call an ambulance.'

His eyes, narrowed with pain, turned to Meyer. 'You fool,' he spat. 'You stupid, greedy, brainless fool!'

Meyer's mouth gaped like a fish. He didn't seem capable of responding to Medlock's insults. He didn't even look as if he knew where he was.

They heard voices and the sound of running feet in the hall. They looked towards the door to see Belinda staring in at them. An instant later, the four policemen came pushing past her.

14   Ganging up

The four girls followed one of the policemen out of the house. He wanted names and home phone numbers from them.

He spoke into his car radio.

'Yes,' he said. 'We're here. It *was* Hawkmoor House. Yes. Everything's under control.' The radio squawked at him and he grinned. 'No, the girl is fine. It wasn't just the one – there are four of them.' He winked at the girls. 'We're going to need an ambulance.' The voice from the other end squawked again. 'No,' the policeman said with a laugh. '*They're* all perfectly fine. It's for the men who did the abducting. They're the ones in need of an ambulance.'

He put the radio back into his car.

'Well, now,' he said. 'Who feels like explaining to me exactly what's been going on here?'

He should have known better. The four excited girls all began talking at once and it was quite a while before the bemused policeman even *began* to be able to make sense of what they were trying to tell him.

And it wasn't until Tracy's mother arrived that the mysterious sudden appearance of the police was explained.

After giving Judy and Tracy a relieved hug she told them the whole story.

'I didn't wake up until the middle of the afternoon,' she said. 'And it was a while after that before I began to worry about where Tracy had got to.' She gave Tracy another hug. 'And then I got that phone call from you,' she continued. 'That was when I *knew* something was wrong. I knew you couldn't have gone off on a bike ride – your bike was in the garden. So I telephoned the police. They came straight over and took me to the station so I could give them the details.'

'That's why your car was still there,' said Belinda. 'We did wonder about that.'

Mrs Foster nodded. 'When I got home afterwards there was a call on the answering machine.'

'From me,' Belinda said proudly.

'Yes,' added Holly drily. 'Telling everyone that Judy was at a place called Haremire House.'

'Anyone can make a simple mistake,' said Belinda. She looked eagerly at Mrs Foster. 'Was it just a wild guess – you know – figuring out that it was really Hawkmoor House?'

'Not exactly,' said Mrs Foster. 'I telephoned the police immediately. It was the police who worked out what you must have meant. Hawkmoor House was the only place nearby that sounded remotely

180

like Haremire. An empty house out in the middle of nowhere.'

The policeman standing nearby nodded. 'We'd had reports of lights in the house at night,' he said. 'We'd just assumed it was tramps or some such, so we hadn't worried about it. We knew the place was derelict. It wasn't until Mrs Foster called us that we put two and two together.' He grinned. 'And arrived just in time to save you doing those poor men any more harm.'

'Poor men!' broke in Judy. 'Meyer had a gun on us. He's as crazy as a polecat. You should have seen the way Tracy jumped on him! Whack! She nearly drove him right through the floor like a nail.'

'And you should have seen the kick Judy gave Medlock,' Tracy said excitedly.

'Yes, yes.' The policeman held his hands up in protest. 'You can all make full statements later. But right now I think you'd all better be getting off home.'

'I'll go along with that,' said Judy. 'I haven't had a wash for days!' Her face became serious. 'Do my folks know about all this?'

'Of course!' exclaimed Mrs Foster. 'You don't know, do you? I don't suppose any of you know.' She looked anxiously at Judy. 'Now, you mustn't worry, dear. But your father has been arrested. Your mother telephoned me to tell me about it.'

'We knew that already,' said Holly. 'Medlock

181

was talking about it at Belinda's mum's party.' She grinned at Judy. 'But it'll all be OK now. He was arrested because they thought he'd stolen the Thai royal jewels. But we've got them back now. They're bound to let him go as soon as they find out.'

'And wait till he hears who was behind it all,' Judy said darkly. 'Tony Meyer!'

Just then the ambulance drew up and they watched as Medlock was carried out on a stretcher. As he was helped into the back of the vehicle, Meyer's eyes glittered briefly with anger and hatred.

They were all very glad that they wouldn't be seeing any more of him.

'Home?' suggested Mrs Foster. She looked at Holly and Belinda. 'You two will have quite a story to tell your parents.'

'I think they're getting used to our adventures,' said Holly with a laugh, as the four girls piled into Mrs Foster's car.

'They ought to be,' added Belinda. 'They've had enough practice, after all!'

The three members of the Mystery Club were sitting in Tracy's garden. A broad coloured parasol shaded them from the blazing sunlight as they sipped lemonade through straws and helped themselves from a large plate piled high with sandwiches.

Protestations from various parents, pointing out the long, exhausting night they had just been through, fell on deaf ears. The girls wanted to get back together as quickly as possible the next day. They had a lot to talk about.

'I still want to know exactly what you told Judy about the Mystery Club,' said Belinda.

'I just told her about the sort of things we get up to,' said Tracy.

'Oh, yes?' replied Belinda, peering at Tracy through her spectacles. 'So why does she think you're our leader?'

Tracy blew some lemonade bubbles down her straw. 'She must have just sort of *assumed* I was. I probably mentioned all the times I've gotten you out of trouble.'

'I bet you did,' said Holly. 'But I don't suppose you bothered telling her all the times we've had to rescue you?'

'Who was it that jumped on Meyer?' said Tracy.

'Yes,' said Belinda. 'And who was it that was dozy enough to get kidnapped by him in the first place?'

'And who was it that decided to give the chocolates to my mum?' said Holly. 'Without even having sense enough to look inside first?'

Tracy leaned over the back of her chair. 'Help!' she shouted into the house. 'Help, Judy! They're ganging up on me.'

But Belinda wasn't to be stopped. 'Who actually

found the necklace?' she said, poking at Tracy with her foot. 'Tell me that.'

'Yes, and took it straight to Meyer.' Tracy laughed. 'All right, all right,' she said. 'I admit it. We *all* did our bit. Just like we always do. The three of us together.'

Judy came bounding down the back steps. 'You're not arguing, are you?' she said brightly. 'You can't be arguing after what we've been through.'

'Want to bet?' said Belinda.

Judy sat in the grass and took a long swig of lemonade. 'I've just spoken to my mom,' she said. 'Dad's OK. Once the police back home heard what had been going on they let him out. Isn't that great? And he's not mad at me any more.' She grinned. 'And I'm not mad at *him* any more. In fact,' she continued with a huge smile, 'Mom and Dad are both coming over here on the first flight they can. Dad's going to pick up the necklace, but they're both going to be stopping in England for at least a week.'

'That's great,' said Tracy. 'It'll be really nice to see them again.' She gave a contented sigh. 'I love happy endings.'

'It's a pity we're all back at school on Monday,' said Belinda gloomily. 'We've wasted most of the half-term holiday chasing around after that necklace.'

'I wouldn't say we *wasted* it, exactly,' said Holly.

'And we've still got a couple of days left.'

'That's right,' said Judy, grinning. 'Plenty of time for some adventures together. Tracy's been telling me about all the amazing things you guys get up to. I can't wait to join in.'

The three friends stared at her.

'Haven't you had enough adventures for one week, Judy?' said Holly.

'I think we'd better make Judy an honorary member of the Mystery Club,' said Belinda with a laugh.

'Good idea,' said Holly. She looked at Tracy. 'And our *first* adventure together can be finding out what flavours of ice-cream Tracy's got in her freezer.'

'Now that,' smiled Belinda, 'is *my* idea of an adventure!'

HIDE AND SEEK

by Fiona Kelly

Holly, Belinda and Tracy are back in the
seventh thrilling adventure in the
Mystery Club series, published by
Knight Books. This time, they meet
up with Holly's friends from Highgate,
Peter and Miranda.

Here is the first chapter . . .

1 An exciting invitation

'How long before we reach London?' Belinda Hayes gazed down through her wire-framed spectacles into her empty lunch box. 'I'm quite peckish.'

She had finished her packed lunch some time ago. Outside the train window the rolling English countryside glided away beneath a glorious blue sky.

Her two friends, Holly Adams and Tracy Foster, looked up at her in despair. She had been asking the same question for the last hour or more.

Tracy had been looking out of the window, passing the time by trying to count the sheep that dotted the fields of nearby farms. She rolled her bright blue eyes and rummaged through her bag, her blonde hair falling around her pretty face. She pulled out an apple.

'Eat this and stop complaining,' she said.

'I wasn't *complaining*,' said Belinda, pushing an unruly lock of dark hair off her face. 'I was just wondering when we'd get there.' She bit into the apple.

Holly, slim and brown haired, tried to get back to reading her book. It was difficult to concentrate with Belinda constantly interrupting.

Belinda nudged Holly with her foot.

'What are you reading?'

'A *book*,' Holly said with a frown. Holly was a voracious reader; her favourites were mystery novels.

'What's it about?' asked Belinda through a mouthful of apple.

'It's about this girl who keeps interrupting someone who is trying to read,' said Holly. 'I've just come to the bit where they go stark raving mad and throw her out of the train window.'

Tracy looked round at her. 'It isn't, is it?'

Holly laughed and closed her book. 'No, of course it isn't.' She looked at her watch. 'We should be at King's Cross Station in about forty-five minutes,' she said. 'Miranda and Peter will be there to meet us, if everything goes according to plan.'

It was an invitation from Holly's old friend Miranda that was bringing the three girls down from the little Yorkshire village of Willow Dale where they lived. Miranda Hunt and Peter Hamilton had been Holly's closest friends during the years when she and her family had lived in Highgate in North London.

Holly and her family had only recently moved from London to Yorkshire, when her mother had taken over the managership of a bank up there, and her father had given up his job as a solicitor to concentrate on his carpentry business.

Apart from her younger brother Jamie, Holly hadn't known anyone at the Winifred Bowen-Davies school. But Holly was quick-witted and intelligent, and it hadn't taken her long to set up the Mystery Club. The intention at first had been for the club members to read, swap and discuss Holly's beloved mystery novels.

Holly's disappointment that only Belinda and Tracy had turned up at the inaugural meeting of the Mystery Club had soon gone away when the three girls became firm friends and found themselves caught up in some very real mysteries.

But, as Holly had said to her two friends, at least there wasn't any mystery about what they'd be getting up to on *this* half-term holiday. They would be sightseeing in London and visiting all the attractions of that huge, exciting city. And to cap it all, Miranda had managed to get them all tickets to see a brand new musical, *The Snow Queen*.

'What's Miranda like?' asked Tracy. The plan was that the three girls would be staying at Miranda's house for the week.

'She's great,' said Holly. 'Really good fun. She was my best friend. Well, they both were, really, Miranda and Peter. Miranda still writes to me every few weeks. Peter doesn't so much, but then boys don't, do they?'

'I wouldn't know,' said Belinda, whose opinion of boys was that if they had four legs and a tail they'd *still* be less interesting than horses. 'Miranda's not one of these sporty types, is she? I mean, she's not some kind of fitness nut, like Tracy here?'

'I am not a *nut*,' said Tracy. 'I'm just not as lazy as you.'

Holly grinned. These exchanges between Belinda and Tracy were just another part of their friendship. Holly thought she would miss the sparring if it ever stopped.

'You'll like her,' Holly said to Belinda. 'She's a bit like you, really. She doesn't care what anyone thinks about her, and she's got a brilliant sense of humour.'

'Oh, no,' said Tracy. 'I don't think I could cope with another Belinda. One's more than enough.'

Belinda beamed. 'I think I like Miranda already,' she said, putting the apple core into her lunch box and sprawling contentedly on the seat. 'How long before we get to London?'

She gave a stifled yelp as the two friends dived at her and tried to cram her travelling bag down over her head.

There was all the usual chaos at King's Cross as the three friends joined the flow of disembarking passengers pouring down towards the ticket barrier. Tracy had two bags and a crammed rucksack weighing her down. Belinda had somehow managed to get all her things into a single hold-all which she was constantly having to apologise for as it bumped against people's legs. Holly had a heavy shoulder-bag and a suitcase. It didn't seem all that long ago when she had packed this same case with clothes on her travels away from London.

Slightly taller than her two friends, Holly craned her neck to see over the bobbing heads, hoping for an early sighting of Peter or Miranda.

She saw Peter first. Tall and skinny with a shock of brown hair falling over his eyes as he stretched his neck over the crowds beyond the barrier.

Holly waved and he waved back. Then she spotted Miranda's long corn-blonde hair and her huge grin and she waved even more frantically.

In another minute or two the five of them were standing among the flood of people on the station concourse and Holly was reeling from a violent hug from the laughing Miranda.

'Brilliant!' said Miranda. 'This is going to be a really great week.' She looked Holly up and down. 'You haven't changed a bit,' she said.

'I've only been gone a few months,' Holly said breathlessly. 'What did you expect? That I'd have grown an extra head or something?'

'I don't know,' said Miranda. 'Yorkshire's a pretty strange place from what you've been telling me.' She grinned at Holly's friends. 'Don't tell me,' she said. '*You're* Belinda, and *you're* Tracy.'

'That's right,' said Tracy.

'You don't sound very American,' Miranda said, looking at Tracy.

'You should hear her when she gets excited,' said Belinda.

'I'm only *half* American,' said Tracy. 'My mom's English.' Tracy had been living in England for three years now, ever since her American father and English mother had got divorced.

'Yes, yes,' said Miranda. 'That's right. I remember. Holly's told me all about both of you in her letters.'

'Really?' said Belinda, giving Holly a suspicious look. 'Such as what?'

'Only nice things,' said Miranda, smiling at Belinda. 'How's your horse? He's called Meltdown, isn't he?'

'That's right,' said Belinda. 'He sends his regards, and says sorry he couldn't make it down for the week, but he's got a gymkhana to train for.'

Miranda gave a startlingly loud yell of laughter. 'I like it,' she said. 'This is going to be fun.'

'I meant to warn you about her laugh,' said Holly with a grin. '*Loud*, isn't it?'

Miranda gave another laugh and linked arms with Holly. 'Let's get off home,' she said. 'We can start planning what we're going to do.' She looked at Tracy and Belinda. 'Have either of you been to London before?'

'I've been *through* it,' said Tracy. 'But I didn't get to see much.'

'That's great,' said Miranda. 'So there's tons to show you. What about you, Belinda?'

'I've been down here a few times,' said Belinda. 'But I've only seen the most obvious bits. You know, the Tower of London and Big Ben and so on.'

'Ahem,' said a quiet voice. Peter was grinning at them. 'Any chance of me getting a word in?'

'Oh, sorry, Peter,' said Holly. 'How are you?'

'I'm fine,' said Peter. 'But I'm just beginning to realise what it's going to be like trying to compete with *four* girls at full throttle. I've made a list of places we could go and see.' He pulled a sheet of paper out of his pocket. 'I've worked it all out on my dad's computer at home. It's all here.'

'Talk about organised,' said Tracy. 'Look at this.' She took the sheet from him. It comprised a long list of tourist attractions in London, divided between the number of days they were going to be there, and sub-divided into the means of getting to them and the times that the journeys would take.

'I've made a list too,' said Holly, pulling the Mystery Club's red notebook out of her shoulder bag. 'We'll have to compare notes.'

'Hang on,' said Belinda. 'This is beginning to

look like hard work.' She read over Tracy's shoulder. 'What's this? The eight o'clock train to Hampton Court?' She looked from Peter to Holly. 'You can cross that one out straightaway. There's no way I'm getting up that early. Don't either of you know what the word *holiday* means?'

'I know what you think it means,' said Holly. 'Lounging about in bed half the morning.'

'Take no notice of Belinda,' said Tracy, smiling at Peter. 'We want to see as much as possible.'

'They were only ideas,' said Peter. 'I thought it would be helpful for us to have a few firm plans to start off with. We don't have to follow it to the letter.'

'Thank heavens for that,' said Belinda.

'We'll have a proper think about it at my place,' said Miranda. 'Shall we go?'

They headed down to the Underground station, pushing their way through the milling crowds.

'Too many people,' puffed Belinda, following Miranda to the machine that dispensed tickets. 'What are they all up to? Don't they have any work to go to?'

'Mostly tourists,' said Miranda with a smile. 'Don't worry. It's only six stops on the Northern Line and we're home.' She fed some money into the machine and pressed a button. 'Keep close to me,' she said. 'We don't want anyone getting lost.'

'Don't worry,' said Belinda, stepping aside as

someone with a colossal rucksack barged past. 'I certainly will.'

Holly walked happily along with her friends, remembering all the adventures she'd had with Peter and Miranda when all three of them had lived in London. It was nice to be back, and Holly was looking forward to showing Belinda and Tracy round all her old haunts.

Miranda lived in a tall terraced house only a five minute walk from the Underground station. She had older twin sisters, Becky and Rachel, who shared a huge attic bedroom. But the twins were away for the week and Belinda and Tracy were to have their room. Holly would be sleeping in with Miranda.

They dumped their bags and went through into the long, bright kitchen with French windows that overlooked a colourful garden.

'Your mum and dad are at work, I suppose?' said Holly.

'Yes,' said Miranda. 'Mum should be back from the office about sixish. I don't think we'll be seeing much of my dad, though. He's been working all hours since he decided to go on his own.' Holly had already learned from Miranda's letters that her father had set up his own advertising agency. Miranda's mother worked as a translator in a government department in Westminster.

Miranda opened the windows and they took

cool drinks out on to the lawn.

'I'm completely free all week,' Miranda told them. 'Except for a couple of nights baby-sitting.' The ice rattled in her glass as she took a swig of lemonade. 'You remember Suzannah Winter, don't you, Holly?'

'The actress friend of your mum?' said Holly. 'Of course I do.' Holly had encountered Suzannah Winter a few times at Miranda's house. She remembered her as being very tall with long dark hair and piercing blue eyes. She also remembered that she had a little daughter, Charlotte.

'Is it Charlotte you're baby-sitting?' asked Holly.

'That's right,' said Miranda. 'Suzannah has got the starring role in that musical I told you about. She's the Snow Queen. That's how I've managed to get our free tickets.'

'Is it a proper West End show?' asked Tracy.

'Not quite,' said Miranda. 'They're staging it at the Hampstead Gardens Theatre at the moment. But if it's a success they're hoping to put it on at one of the big theatres in the West End.'

'I didn't know you knew any actresses,' Belinda said to Holly. 'Suzannah Winter? Should I know her? Is she famous? I mean, has she been in any films?'

'She mostly works in the theatre,' said Peter. 'But this is the first major role she's had for about six years, apparently. It's her big come-back after taking time off to look after Charlotte. She's got one of the cast staying with her.'

'Oh, yes,' said Miranda. 'Gail. Gail Farrier. She's renting a room in Suzannah's house while her own flat is being decorated or something. She's only got a small part. She's one of Suzannah's ice maidens.'

'What's she like?' asked Tracy.

'Gail? I don't know much about her,' said Miranda. 'She's very quiet. I haven't seen much of her, really. I don't think Charlotte likes her, though. Gail calls Charlotte "Lottie", and Charlotte can't stand that. She might only be five, but she's got very definite ideas about what she likes.' She smiled at the others. 'She's a really nice kid, though.'

'We wouldn't mind coming baby-sitting with you for a couple of evenings, so long as Suzannah doesn't mind us all turning up,' said Holly. She looked at Tracy and Belinda. 'We wouldn't mind, would we?'

'Of course we wouldn't,' said Tracy. 'We can't leave Miranda all on her own.'

'I'm not sure I'm very good with children,' said Belinda. 'I don't even know which way up you're supposed to hold them.'

Miranda gave a yell of laughter. 'Feet downwards usually does the trick,' she said. 'But it'd be great if you really don't mind. Suzannah's got heaps of videos we can watch, and she always fills the fridge with food and drinks for me. I'm sure she won't mind you all coming along. I'm baby-sitting Charlotte this evening. I'll give Suzannah a ring to make sure it's all right to bring you all with me.'

'I'm really busy this evening,' said Peter. 'I'm working on a car with a couple of friends.' He grinned ruefully at them. 'Sorry, but you'll have to count me out of baby-sitting.'

'Coward,' said Miranda. 'He's just scared of Charlotte, that's all it is.'

'Wise man,' said Belinda.

Holly stood up. 'Does anyone fancy a quick wander round the area? I can show you where I used to live.'

'I'll come with you,' said Peter. 'Then I'm going to have to head off home.'

'OK,' said Miranda. 'You lot go for a stroll. If you three get back here for about five o'clock, we'll have something to eat before going off to Suzannah's.'

Peter and the three girls headed off.

The main streets were busy and filled with traffic.

'Everyone seems in such a hurry,' said Belinda. 'Like a load of ants rushing around. And it's so noisy. Aren't there any quiet bits?'

'There are parks,' said Peter. 'And it's quieter in the back streets.' He shrugged. 'I don't really notice it, to be honest.'

'I like it,' said Tracy. 'It's lively. Like there's lots

going on. Are you going to show us where you lived, Holly?'

They made their way from the bustle of the main streets into a more peaceful residential area.

Holly showed them the house that her family had lived in.

'I wish I could have a look inside,' she said. 'I'd like to know what the new people have done with it.'

'You're probably better off not knowing,' said Belinda.

A few streets away they came to Peter's house.

'See you in the morning,' he said. 'Have a nice evening baby-sitting, won't you?'

As the three girls walked away, Holly told them a few things about Peter. He lived alone with his father, who was a lecturer at a nearby college. His mother had died when Peter was very young.

'Poor thing,' said Tracy. 'I'd be lost without my mom.'

Holly took them on a long detour that she told them would eventually bring them back to Miranda's house.

'Is Horse Guards Parade on our sightseeing list?' asked Belinda. 'I'd like to see some horses.'

'We'll go through our lists this evening,' said Holly. 'Peter left his with me. Between us we should be able to sort out plenty of interesting places to go.'

'I want to go to Madame Tussaud's,' said Tracy. 'And the Planetarium.'

'Will we have time for the zoo?' asked Belinda.

'I wouldn't go there if I were you,' Tracy said, grinning. 'They might not let you out again.'

'I was thinking the same about you and the waxworks,' said Belinda. 'They've got a Chamber of Horrors in there. They might think you're an exhibit.'

'They do bus tours,' said Holly with a laugh. 'They even have open-topped buses. Perhaps we should go on one of those?'

They talked cheerfully as they made their way back to Miranda's house. The four girls had a quick meal before catching a bus for the short ride to Suzannah Winter's house.

Suzannah lived in a wide tree-lined crescent of detached houses with long, elegant front gardens.

As they rounded the corner, chatting and laughing in the warmth of the early evening, Miranda suddenly came to a halt.

Further along the gently curving road a dark blue four-door car was parked by the kerb. It was facing away from them. There was a man at the wheel and standing by the open door was a policewoman talking to another woman.

Holly recognised Suzannah Winter immediately. Tall and slender in a long black coat, her dark hair hanging halfway down her back, her sharply beautiful face lined with concern.

'I wonder what's going on?' said Miranda.

'There's one way to find out,' said Belinda.

As the four girls walked along to where Suzannah Winter was standing, the policewoman got into the car and it drove away.

'Is anything wrong?' asked Miranda.

Suzannah looked distractedly at them. 'Yes, I'm afraid there is,' she said, staring after the car.

Her piercing blue eyes turned to the four silent girls.

'Come inside,' she said. 'And I'll tell you all about it.'

They followed her up the path. At the door she stopped and looked round at them. 'They were looking for Gail,' she said as the girls gazed at her in amazement. 'They came here to arrest her!'

TITLES AVAILABLE IN THE
MYSTERY CLUB SERIES

All Hodder Children's books are available at your local bookshop or newsagent, or can be ordered direct from the publisher. Just tick the titles you want and fill in the form below. Prices and availability subject to change without notice.

Hodder Children's Books, Cash Sales Department, Bookpoint, 39 Milton Park, Abingdon, OXON, OX14 4TD, UK. If you have a credit card you may order by telephone – (01235) 400414.

Please enclose a cheque or postal order made payable to Bookpoint Ltd to the value of the cover price and allow the following for postage and packing:
UK & BFPO – £1.00 for the first book, 50p for the second book, and 30p for each additional book ordered up to a maximum charge of £3.00.
OVERSEAS & EIRE – £2.00 for the first book, £1.00 for the second book, and 50p for each additional book.

Name...

Address...

....

....

If you would prefer to pay by credit card, please complete:
Please debit my Visa/Access/Diner's Card/American Express (delete as applicable) card no:

Signature...

Expiry Date..